"How much do you want for her?"

Lidi stared at Scabbia. "What are you talking about?"

"The child." Scabbia twitched impatiently. "The child. What price?"

Lidi had trouble believing what she was hearing. She had, at first, taken him for an infuriating nuisance. She decided he was an infuriating lunatic.

"There isn't a price. Nobody's for sale."

"There's always a price. Everything has a price."

"Not everything." Lidi turned away. Scabbia kept after her, nearly treading on her heels. The more she tried to shake him off, the more he clutched at her...

———

"The undercurrent of melancholy running beneath (and occasionally bursting to the surface of) this fanciful tale makes it as memorable as Alexander's previous Chronicles of Prydain and Westmark Trilogy.... Even as the outsize characterizations and rollicking adventure amuse, the compassionate vision of life's possibilities is likely to bring a lump to the throat." —*Publishers Weekly*

"Ever a wizard with words, Alexander imbues this tale of a young magician on a quest with whiffs of mystery." —*School Library Journal*

BOOKS BY LLOYD ALEXANDER

The Prydain Chronicles

The Book of Three

The Black Cauldron

The Castle of Llyr

Taran Wanderer

The High King

The Foundling

The Westmark Trilogy

Westmark

The Kestrel

The Beggar Queen

The Vesper Holly Adventures

The Illyrian Adventure

The El Dorado Adventure

The Drackenberg Adventure

The Jedera Adventure

The Philadelphia Adventure

LLOYD ALEXANDER

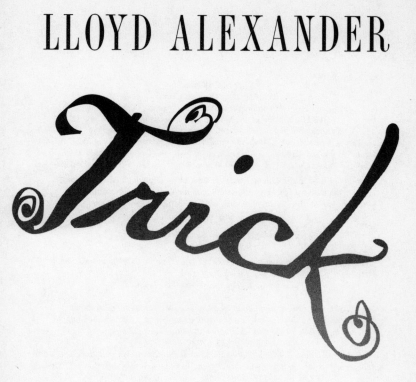

Trick

PUFFIN BOOKS

PUFFIN BOOKS

Published by Penguin Group

Penguin Young Readers Group,

345 Hudson Street, New York, New York 10014, U.S.A.

Penguin Books Ltd, 80 Strand, London WC2R ORL, England

Penguin Books Australia Ltd, 250 Camberwell Road, Camberwell, Victoria 3124, Australia

Penguin Books Canada Ltd, 10 Alcorn Avenue, Toronto, Ontario, Canada M4V 3B2

Penguin Books (N.Z.) Ltd, 182-190 Wairau Road, Auckland 10, New Zealand

First published in the United States of America by Dutton Children's Books,
a division of Penguin Putnam Books for Young Readers, 2002
Published by Puffin Books, a division of Penguin Young Readers Group, 2004

3 5 7 9 10 8 6 4

THE LIBRARY OF CONGRESS HAS CATALOGED THE DUTTON EDITION AS FOLLOWS:

Alexander, Lloyd.

The rope trick / by Lloyd Alexander—1st ed.

p. cm.

Summary: Motivated by her quest to learn a legendary rope trick,
the magician Princess Ledi and her troupe embark on a journey through
Renaissance Italy that intertwines adventure, love, and mystery.

ISBN: 0-525-47020-4 (hc)

[1. Magicians—Fiction. 2. Magic tricks—Fiction. 3. Adventure and adventurers—Fiction.
4. Theater—Fiction. 5. Supernatural—Fiction. 6. Italy—History—Fiction.] I. Title.

PZ7.A 3774 Ro 2002 [Fic]—dc21 2002067497

Puffin Books ISBN 0-14-240119-6

Printed in the United States of America

For those in search of
their own magic

Contents

1

Zaccovelli's Nose

LIDI WAS NOT EASY TO IGNORE, especially when flame shot out of her fingertips. Also, she had an attractive smile. "Remember to smile a lot," Jericho once told her. "It shows people you know what you're doing. They like that."

Raindrops the size of grapes pelted down. It should not have been so chilly this time of year in Campania. The wind had fishtailed around and started blowing from the north. It would stop in a couple of days, but Lidi had no time to lose. Jericho was waiting. They needed the money.

Every town had some kind of inn or tavern. She had seen dozens, all much the same. She stepped through the door of the first one she came to. The signboard read *Albergo Zaccovelli*.

It was no different from the others: noisy and stifling, smelling of charcoal embers, damp clothing, and sour wine. Town idlers, maybe twenty, lounged at trestle tables, eating, drinking, arguing over cards or dominoes. The grease and smoke coating the ceiling looked thick enough to keep the roof from crashing down. Her father had died in a place like this.

"*Ecco!* Here, look!" She clapped her hands. "See Princess Lidi and her magical mystifications!"

She shook her arms free of the cloak and tossed her hat to the floor, where it clearly waited for coins. She was not stunningly beautiful. She could be pretty when she felt like it. Her hair, in any case, was spectacular, a mass of curls, shining, copper-colored, tumbling to her waist. She decided to begin with "Hands of Glory." She spread her fingers. Puffs of smoke and jets of blue flame spurted from them. Lidi had done the effect a thousand times. It was ridiculously easy, but it got immediate attention.

This time, not exactly as she wanted. The idlers stiffened on their benches. They were startled, even frightened, but all of the same mind: Here was a girl, a total stranger, shooting fire at them. Since she could not be overlooked, they did the next best thing: Pretend nothing happened. If they admitted anything extraordinary was going on, they might have to do something about it. They glanced around in every direction but hers and studied the local flies. Let Zaccovelli deal with her.

A moment later, Zaccovelli himself hurried up. He

squinted at Lidi. His head looked too heavy for his neck. Bigger and rounder than a Campania melon, the kind without ridges, it kept tilting from one side to the other.

"What, are you a crazy person?" Zaccovelli shouted. "*Pazza!* You want to burn down my house?"

His first intention was to throw her out. But in view of Lidi's fingers blazing like torches, Zaccovelli felt uneasy and not certain how to go about doing that. Yelling seemed a good way to begin.

Lidi smiled and closed her hands. The flames vanished. "No, I'm not a crazy person. I don't want to burn down your house. I want to put money in your pocket."

Zaccovelli quit yelling.

"I do a show for your customers," Lidi said in his ear. "They stay longer, they spend more. Simple."

Zaccovelli hesitated. Without waiting for his answer, out of nowhere Lidi suddenly produced a red silk scarf. She waved it back and forth. It turned into a deck of cards.

Lidi pretended to be surprised. "How did this get here?"

She pulled out a card. "What's this? Why, it's His Majesty, the king of hearts."

She held it up for all to see. With a snap of her wrist, she skimmed it into the air. It spun, circled a moment, then flew straight down into the middle of the deck.

"The king always likes to be next to the queen." Lidi fanned open the deck to show the two side by side. She passed a hand over the cards and they were gone.

Zaccovelli's customers, by now, had chewed over and

digested the matter. Carnival trickery, though better than they had ever seen; and the girl had nice hair.

"Do that again," somebody called.

Lidi had already done a trick better than turning a scarf into a deck of cards. She had turned idle gapers into an audience—except for Zaccovelli, who had gone to stand by his counter and was keeping a sour eye on her. The crowd began clapping. Coins were thrown into the hat.

Lidi set about her business. Her big illusions needed more equipment. She would have to do sleight of hand. In a room this small, people might try to come too close, drift around where she didn't want them to be, or jostle her into making mistakes. Jericho, her canvasmaster, reassured her. "Don't worry," he said, "they won't notice how you do it. They don't want to notice, they want to be mystified. Slip up, you cover it. You know how. Make them think they're seeing miracles. They'll forgive your mistakes."

Jericho prided himself on his hard head and tough skin, so what he said next took her by surprise.

"One big thing," Jericho said. "You have to love them."

Lidi went through the usual sleights. She produced, for example, a length of rope. She cut it in half with a pocket-knife and tossed the pieces in the air. The rope came down whole again. She fished out three white balls from her cloak, set them between her fingers. They turned red, then blue, before vanishing into nowhere. Common tricks, the stock-in-trade of every down-at-the-heels charlatan standing on a barrel at a country fair. She could have done them in her sleep.

What made them different was: Lidi. Her hands, to begin with, remarkable even for a magician's; slender, supple, and quite beautiful. All eyes followed wherever she gestured. Nobody noticed that her other hand was busy getting ready for the next effect. And then, her voice. She kept up a bright stream of patter, joking, teasing, hinting at wonders to come, flirting a little when she needed to. Whoever listened forgot such boring nonsense as the laws of physics. The impossible became perfectly natural.

She did a few more sleights. She realized the shower of coins had begun drying up. There were more cheers than cash. The moment had come to make a clean exit. She decided to close with the "The Miser's Dream."

Lidi picked up her hat, rummaged around in it, and turned it upside down. She frowned, puzzled to find it empty—as she knew it would be, since she had tucked the money under the flap of a hidden pocket in the lining.

"Lost? Strayed? Never mind," she said while the audience gasped. "I can always find more."

A coin materialized between her thumb and forefinger. She dropped it into the hat. She did likewise as a dozen more appeared, one after the other. The onlookers stared, convinced she could have gone on plucking money out of the air for days on end. Which she could have done, for it was the same coin deftly palmed again and again, never leaving her fingers.

Zaccovelli had been leaning on his counter, watching. It had taken him a while, but he finally worked it out. Every penny his customers spent on Lidi meant a penny less they spent on food and drink. He stepped over to her. Zaccovelli was not in good humor.

"Whatever you've got in that hat," he said, "I want my fair share." He had already calculated something on the order of a thirty-seventy split. In his favor.

Lidi upended the hat and showed it to him empty.

"That's odd," she said. "It was all here a minute ago."

She reached out and pulled a coin from his nose.

She shouldn't have done it. Zaccovelli was too angry to enjoy the effect. Out of sheer mischief or amusement, she did it anyhow. She should have known better. According to Jericho, the biggest mistakes are made by people who should know better.

The customers laughed. Zaccovelli did not.

"Let's have the money and no nonsense." Zaccovelli was a practical man, as he had to be in his line of work. He knew trickery when he saw it. At the same time, stronger than reason, he halfway believed Lidi had actually plucked the coin from his nostril.

"Hand that over," Zaccovelli said. "Since it came out of my nose, it belongs to me."

This was the first time anyone had made such a demand. The piece was real silver; Lidi used it specially for "The Miser's Dream" because it glittered nicely. She had no intention of giving it away.

Zaccovelli's melon of a head wobbled so far to one side that he was viewing her almost horizontally. "Give it here."

"Of course." Lidi shrugged. "If you insist."

"I insist," Zaccovelli said.

"I'll put it back where I got it," Lidi said.

She made a quick pass toward the innkeeper's nose. The silver coin disappeared. Zaccovelli sneezed and sputtered as if it had in fact shot into the deep recesses of his skull. He clapped his hands to his face and rubbed hard. Whether he believed money would come streaming from his nose, whether the piece had lodged forever in some unreachable area, or whether it was all a fraud, he was thoroughly confused and baffled.

While his customers guffawed at his antics, Zaccovelli began smacking one ear, like a swimmer trying to rid himself of water in the other.

Lidi took this moment to set her money-laden hat firmly on her head. She flung her cloak around her shoulders, and with a hasty bow of gratitude toward her audience, she swept out the door.

The rain had slackened. Twilight was gathering over the empty streets. Jericho had parked both wagons just beyond the piazza, along with the two big draft horses. He was her canvasmaster, as he had been her father's, in charge of pitching the tent and setting up the platform. Until a couple of months ago, he had a few roustabouts to help with the lifting and hauling. They had, one by one, drifted away, looking for regular wages. Jericho stayed.

Lidi picked her way around the puddles. She heard a *slap-slap-slap* on the wet cobblestones behind her. She glanced back, wondering if Zaccovelli was coming after her. She saw no one. She hurried across the open square.

The quick *slap-slap-slap* continued. Lidi stopped short and turned around. As best she could make out through the drizzle, she was being followed by a burlap sack with a pair of skinny legs.

2

Sometimes Daniella

LIDI WAS TOO CURIOUS TO TURN AWAY. The sack also had arms, and a rope tied around the middle. There seemed to be a head, though it was more like a rag mop, dripping and clotted, that someone had forgotten to wring out. The slapping noise came from two bare feet on the wet cobbles. It was a person, more or less.

Lidi waited. The sack and its contents moved steadily toward her. When it came within a pace of Lidi, it stopped. It was a child; a small girl, given the benefit of the doubt.

Lidi put her hands on her hips. The girl did the same. The two of them stood watching each other.

"What do you want?" Lidi finally said.

The girl shrugged.

"Are you lost?" Lidi said.

"No. I'm found."

Even in the dark, the girl's eyes shone as if lit from inside; and so big and round, they took up her whole face. Lidi had seen that look before.

"Grub?" Lidi said. "Is that it?"

The girl held out a grimy hand. Lidi took it in her own, so naturally that she didn't realize she was doing it until after she had done it. "You have a name?"

"Mostly they call me 'stupid idiot,'" the girl said. "Sometimes Daniella."

"Come on, then," Lidi said.

The wagons stood a few streets away from the piazza. One was the tent wagon, high-sided, roofed over with heavy tarpaulins. It held rolls of canvas, poles, pegs, and all the other gear needed to pitch a tent. The side of the wagon could swing down and turn into a platform. Jericho drove this vehicle and slept in it at night. The other, the property wagon, was a wooden house on big wheels: Lidi's quarters, where she also kept her stage equipment and costumes.

Jericho sat on the short flight of steps leading up to the door of the property wagon. He was tall, barrel-chested, with a face the color of a walnut shell and as hard. A red bandanna covered his gray hair, nearly as closely shaven as his chin and cheeks. Jericho kept his hair short because he often doubled as a juggler of flaming torches, and he wanted to avoid setting his head on fire. He could swallow swords if he had to, though he would rather not. It gave him indigestion.

As soon as he caught sight of Lidi, Jericho climbed down from the steps. He was soaking wet. Lidi knew he had been waiting all this time in the rain.

He cocked a dark eye at the girl dressed in a sack. "What's this?"

"Sometimes Daniella," Lidi said.

The child giggled. "You're being silly. 'Sometimes' isn't part of it."

"I brought her," Lidi said.

"Why?"

"She wants something to eat," Lidi said.

"Who doesn't?" Jericho said. "This is not a good idea. Feed her once, she'll never go away. Like a stray cat."

Grumbling and muttering to himself, the canvasmaster nevertheless gently helped the girl up the steps and into the property wagon. It was snug inside and well arranged. Lidi's folding cot was set against one wall. An oil lamp hung from the ceiling. There were crowded shelves, stacks of brightly painted chests and boxes. Part of the property wagon, separated by a curtain, was given over to Lidi's special equipment. There was still room enough for a tiny charcoal stove and several collapsible stools. Daniella immediately went and perched on one of the stools, where her spindly legs dangled.

Jericho took a sausage from the tin basin on the stove. "Here."

"I ate a sausage once," Daniella said. "It wasn't like this."

"You complain about my cooking?" Jericho said.

"No," Daniella said. "Mine was different. It was green."

Somebody began pounding on the door. In the closed space of the wagon, it made a terrible racket. Lidi started up. Daniella stopped devouring the sausage in mid-bite.

"Who the devil—?" Jericho barely had time to open the door. Zaccovelli flung himself inside. He flapped his arms and shook his fists. His head wobbled furiously.

"Kidnapper!" he shouted at Lidi as Daniella shrank into herself and sat frozen on the stool. "She was watching you from the kitchen. I saw her duck out. I followed her, the little wretch. What do you think you're doing? I'll have the law on you."

Zaccovelli was so busy yelling at Lidi that he did not at first notice Jericho, who took hold of him by the shirtfront.

"Shut up," Jericho said quietly but in a tone that made Zaccovelli choke. "Whoever you are, I don't want to hear gabble about the law."

"I know him," Lidi said. "He keeps the inn here."

Zaccovelli wiggled free of the canvasmaster. He pointed a finger at Daniella. "She's mine."

Lidi frowned and glanced at Daniella. "True? He's your father?"

Daniella's mouth opened and shut. No words came from it, only gagging noises. Her face had gone pale under the coating of grime.

"Her father? Don't insult me," Zaccovelli said. "I picked her out of the gutter. Pure kindness. The goodness of my heart. I taught her all she knows. Pot scrubbing, floor mopping, everything. She's valuable property now. I'll have her back."

Daniella's eyes went to Lidi. They were sea green and wide open, pleading wordlessly. The rest of her face was pinched; her lips trembled.

"We could talk about this," Lidi said.

"Talk? Talk?" Zaccovelli burst out. "What's to talk?"

Lidi raised a hand as he started for Daniella. "Money. What else?"

Jericho stepped protectively closer to Daniella.

Lidi continued: "She's valuable? Worth something? The question is: How much?"

"Ah, signorina . . ." Zaccovelli became suddenly polite. "That would have to be calculated."

"Go on," Lidi said. "Calculate."

"Yes. Well, now, I've had her a year. More or less, give or take a little," Zaccovelli said as Lidi raised a questioning eyebrow. "I can be easy about that. Still, signorina, I've had to put food in her belly, clothes on her back—"

"A bag," Lidi said.

"*Va bene,* I'll throw that in for free," Zaccovelli said. "The rest—all her meals, lodging, incidental expenses—"

"So you claim," Lidi broke in. "I should believe anything you tell me?"

Zaccovelli laid a hand on the general vicinity of his heart. "A humble innkeeper, a poor but honest man, signorina."

"That strikes the eye. You positively radiate," Lidi said. "Yes, you deserve to be paid for your time and trouble, every penny they're worth. I'll make you an offer."

Zaccovelli got himself ready to turn down any sum that Lidi named and insist on three times the amount. The idea that an offer would be made at all put him in a comfortable frame of mind. "Whatever's reasonable."

"Here's what I'll do for you." Lidi took a piece of paper and a pencil stub from a shelf. She handed them to Zaccovelli. "You're a man of business, quick at figures. I want you to write down a line of four single numbers. All different. Don't tell me what they are. Don't let me see them."

Zaccovelli put the paper on his knee and cupped one hand over it. He scribbled a lot more than the price he intended to demand. In lire: 9,754. Close to an astronomical sum. So he had room to dicker. Things were going better than he had expected.

"Write those numbers in reverse order," Lidi said, and waited for him to do it.

"Now," she said, "subtract the smaller amount from the larger."

"What nonsense is this? You take me for a schoolboy?" Zaccovelli had set down 4,579 and came up with a result of 5,175.

"Nearly done," Lidi said. "Now add each of those last four numbers together.

"There's no way I could know the final number you wrote. Impossible," she went on as Zaccovelli bobbled his head.

"But," she said, "if by some lucky chance I tell you that number, that's how much I'll pay. If I'm wrong, I'll give you whatever you ask. Fair enough?"

Zaccovelli nodded eagerly, surprised that Lidi was such a fool but happy to agree. "A bargain."

Lidi closed her eyes and put her hands on her forehead. She frowned deeply. "Too hard. I'm not getting the answer. I can't see it in my mind. I'm sorry I ever thought I could do it."

"Too bad for you," Zaccovelli said. "You won't back out of it now."

"Give me another moment," Lidi said. "Something's coming to me. Probably wrong, but the best I can do.

"The number," she said, after some hesitation, "the number is—eighteen."

Zaccovelli gulped. Lidi took the paper from him. "Imagine that! Exactly what you wrote. Amazing! So, I'll give you eighteen lire. Not much. I'm sorry it isn't more. I guess I was just lucky."

"Oh, no, you won't get away with that," Zaccovelli blurted as Lidi took eighteen coins from her hat. "You swindled me! I don't know how, but I won't stand for it."

"Yes, you will," put in Jericho, laying a heavy hand on Zaccovelli's neck. "A bargain's a bargain. Do you want to discuss it with me? Otherwise, get out of here."

Zaccovelli jumped to his feet and snatched the money from Lidi's outstretched palm. "Cheats! Thieves, both of you!" He started for the door, then turned back.

"You think you got the better of me?" he shouted. He raised the hand holding the coins and shook it triumphantly. "Ha! You criminals, I got the better of you. The little idiot isn't worth half this. She's worth nothing. She's damaged in the brain, witless, not all there. She can't even speak. You're welcome to her, and you can all go to the devil."

Zaccovelli slammed the door after him. Jericho chuckled. "Well done," he said. "Princess, you can still make me laugh with that old trick. You almost had me believing you didn't know the number."

"It's always eighteen," Daniella said.

3

Princess Lidi

"IT COMES TO EIGHTEEN EVERY TIME." Daniella had hunched up her shoulders and squeezed her arms around herself. She looked in danger of disappearing into the burlap sack. Now sure that Zaccovelli was gone, she relaxed, kicked her heels against the legs of the stool, and grinned at Lidi and Jericho.

Lidi was not used to being surprised; she was the one who surprised other people. She stared at Daniella. "How do you know?"

"Easy," Daniella said. "I thought of a lot of numbers and how they worked out. It was always the same."

"You did it in your head? Just like that?" Lidi said.

"Can't everybody?" Daniella said.

"No." Lidi had heard of people with a knack for that sort of calculation. She had never met any. "Maybe one in a million. What else can you do like that?"

"I don't know." Daniella shrugged. "I never tried it before."

Lidi did not pursue the question. Something else puzzled her. "Why did Zaccovelli say you couldn't speak?"

"He didn't know I could," Daniella said. "After he got me, I never talked."

"Not hard to understand," Jericho said under his breath to Lidi. "Scared. Too scared even to run away. She shut up tight as a clam. I'd say she's been knocked around pretty hard. Enough to beat the words out of anybody."

Daniella turned her full attention to the interrupted sausage. It took her no time to finish it. She licked the tin basin, then licked her fingers. She yawned and gave a little girl's happy belch.

Jericho drew Lidi aside. "Now what?"

"She can sleep in my cot," Lidi said. "That should be a novelty for her."

Daniella had already dozed off. She was oblivious to Lidi settling her on the canvas sling. Jericho came to glance down at her.

"She can't stay here," he said.

Lidi nodded. "I know that."

"You want to keep her anyway."

"Don't you?"

Jericho wished she hadn't asked him that question. He was a large man, and if anybody in Lidi's audience got out of hand, Jericho had only to go and stand next to the trouble-maker, who immediately grew quiet. Jericho was a tiger when it came to protecting Lidi, but she was the only one. He had a secret. He was softhearted. He did everything he could to hide it, even avoiding sick dogs, stray cats, and wounded birds. He knew the world well enough to fear that this might be used against him. Lidi had found out his secret years ago.

"You'll want to give her a good scrubbing in the morning," Jericho said. "She'll need clothes, too."

"I'll find some of my old ones."

Daniella, who had been sound asleep, was sitting upright, eyes open, fixed on Jericho. Her face was calm.

"You," Daniella said, in a casual tone. "You dug a hole and put a man in it."

Jericho's head snapped back. After a moment, he said, "So what if I did? What's that to you?"

"It's all right." Daniella smiled. "He was dead."

She lay down and went to sleep again as if she had never been awake.

"How the devil did she come up with that?" Jericho said.

"I don't know." Lidi, surprised for the second time, peered down at Daniella, who was snuffling peacefully. "But it's true."

Neither said anything more. Neither had anything useful to say. Jericho went, brooding, to the tent wagon. Lidi sat watching the sleeping child.

Lidi felt like a member of her own audience, mystified by a trick that had, in fact, a simple explanation. Whatever that explanation was, Daniella had been right. Six months before, they were getting ready to leave one of the northern towns—like so many of the others, its named blurred in her memory, but it had a sunny, open field. Lidi was sitting on the steps of the property wagon. It was already full morning, but her father had still not come back from the local tavern. Jericho, impatient, had gone looking for him. After a while, she saw Jericho and a man in a stained apron. Between them, they carried a wooden shutter. Her father lay full-length on the slotted board. She had seen this often enough.

This time, Jericho's face was hard-set. They put the shutter and its burden on the grass near the tent wagon. Lidi went to them. Jericho glanced at her and shook his head.

She understood her father was dead. She did not cry, only pressed her face against Jericho's chest. The man in the apron mentioned some small considerations to be dealt with. Jericho nodded and gave him money.

They still had, in those days, a couple of roustabouts traveling with them, but Jericho dug the grave himself. He did it quietly and neatly.

"What now?" he said later. He motioned toward the wagons. "All yours. It's up to you."

"Move on." She did not ask if Jericho would stay with her. She did not need to.

She had known the canvasmaster for as long as she could remember, and better than her own mother: a northern woman who only gave Lidi copper-colored hair, walked away one day, and never came back.

After that, her father gradually grew less interested in performing. And less able. His hands shook, he was too befuddled even to do "The Miser's Dream." He trained Lidi to be his assistant and taught her to do his tricks and effects. She learned quickly, which for some reason put him in a blacker mood. He taunted her when she made a mistake and often when she didn't.

"A magician? You? No real magician until you can do the rope trick. You never will."

"I will, too," Lidi flung back at him. "I'll learn it and I'll be a better magician than you ever were. I'll be the best."

He would try to hit her then. "Best at nothing."

She could dodge the blows but not the words.

———

Several days after the burial, Jericho repainted the lettering that covered the sides of the wagons. He had found pots of red and yellow paint and some scraggy brushes.

"Like to be a princess?" he asked her.

Lidi shrugged. "Good as anything."

The lettering, with fancy curlicues, read MARIO'S MAGICAL MYSTIFICATIONS. Jericho set about painting over MARIO so he could replace it with PRINCESS LIDI.

It was only then that she began to cry.

"Listen to me." Jericho put down the brush. "He wasn't a happy man. Let it go at that.

"I'm surprised you put up with him," he added. "I expected you'd have run off long ago."

"He needed me," Lidi said. "Now he doesn't."

4

In Campania

THE RAIN STOPPED AT DAWN. Daniella was still asleep. Whatever other startling talents she had, she could also smile and snore at the same time. Lidi, who had slept sitting up, went and roused Jericho. The outlying fields would be ankle-deep in mud, impossible to pitch the tent there; and she had no intention of putting on a show in the piazza. She only wanted to be gone in case the innkeeper had any thoughts about making trouble.

Later in the morning, when they were well on their way, Lidi waved for Jericho to pull up. They parked by the roadside. Jericho hauled buckets of water from a creek he found nearby and helped Lidi fill the laundry tub. He went to look after the horses and make something to eat.

Daniella, meantime, had popped out of the property wagon. She was clear-eyed, in good spirits. She said not a word about anything that had happened the night before, as if all had been forgotten. Lidi thought it best not to remind the child. For the moment, she concentrated on scrubbing her, amazed at how many layers of dirt had to be scraped away. Daniella happily splashed and giggled.

It took time, but Lidi discovered the child had sandy hair, not soot-colored, and a pale skin, mostly unscarred. Seeing her clean and happy, Lidi would have liked to think of her as a butterfly coming out of a grimy cocoon. But Daniella was hardly a butterfly. Dressed in the odds and ends of clothing Lidi rummaged out and pinned to fit, she now looked like any everyday underfed and undergrown ragamuffin; for her, a step up in the world.

The canvasmaster had fried some slabs of polenta, the eternal cornmeal mush favored in these northern provinces. He openly grumbled that it would have made better paving for the roads; secretly, he had a taste for it. Daniella wolfed down her portion and skipped off to look at the draft horses.

"Another mouth to feed," Jericho said, when the child was out of earshot.

"A small mouth," Lidi said.

"It will get bigger."

"We'll still feed it," Lidi said. "She reminds me of someone I used to know. Me."

"No doubt," Jericho said. "I've been thinking about her. I once saw a fellow in a carnival show. If you told him the year and date you were born, he'd tell you what day of the week it was, quick as snapping your fingers. Find out what else she can do with numbers and such. She might be an added attraction."

"No." Lidi shook her head. "They used her like a dumb animal. We'd be doing the same. No. I won't."

Jericho poked at the fire with the toe of his boot. As much as he agreed with Lidi, for her sake he had to be practical. "Another act could help. Until you learn that rope trick. If you ever do."

"Once I see it, I can figure out how it works. It's only a trick. The best in the world, but a trick all the same."

The illusion was called "Climb to the Sky." This was what brought Lidi to Campania in the first place. Her father had talked about it a lot: The performer pulled a long rope from a big wicker basket and tossed it full-length into the air. It stayed upright. The magician shinnied up the rope to the very end and vanished in a puff of smoke. The rope went slack and fell to the ground. An instant later, he sprang out of the basket.

Everyone in the profession had heard of it. Like other artists, they were seldom impressed by a colleague's work. In this case, though, they agreed it was amazing.

There were two difficulties. First, few had actually seen it with their own eyes. Second, only one person had ever been known to do it: a magician calling himself "The Fantastic Ferramondo."

Often, half in a stupor, her father babbled that only the rope trick could save them. He had, in a feckless way, been trying to track down the magician. Lidi went at it obsessively, just as she had endlessly practiced card tricks and rolling coins across her knuckles. She had a clue. Her father had muttered about a town in the south of Campania: Montalto.

"You're a fine magician already," Jericho said. "Better than your father even at his best. You don't need a piece of rope to make your fortune."

"It has nothing to do with making a fortune," Lidi said. "It's more than that. It's something I want, something I need to have. For myself."

"That's as may be," Jericho said. "Even so, be practical. You could do very well if you'd give more performances. If you'd spend your time working up your programs instead of this wild-goose chase."

"It's my only goose," Lidi said. "The only goose worth chasing."

She did not realize Daniella had been listening until the girl put her chin on Lidi's shoulder.

"I want to be an added attraction," Daniella said.

Lidi turned to look at her. "You have big ears. Did you hear what I told Jericho? No. You won't be. That's decided."

"Yes, I will," Daniella said. "I *am* the added attraction."

She danced away to the property wagon before Lidi could answer.

———

As it turned out, Daniella had her way. By inattention more than anything else. For the next several days, they rode deeper into Campania. Farther south, the weather softened.

The air even smelled better. Here were olive trees with silvery leaves, and the greenest foliage Lidi had ever seen.

Campania—in a practical sense, there was no such country. A slender stretch of land reached like a woman's graceful arm into the sea. Mapmakers, whose occupation was naming and measuring every inch of ground everywhere, called it "Campania." For their own convenience. As a country, it did not exist. Instead, there was a crowd of provinces, duchies, free cities, pocket-size republics, and hidden corners with no name at all: such a geographical crazy quilt the mapmakers never figured out exactly where one began and another ended.

Lidi had no idea how many of these provinces she would have to pass through. Each had its own style. In some, the women dressed in black, the men paraded around like peacocks in rainbow-colored shirts and striped knee breeches; in others, the women were decked out in scarves and sashes and billowing skirts, while the men wore tight-fitting dark velveteen suits. In any case, Lidi followed the same plan. If a town looked prosperous, she and Jericho would halt the wagons in the middle of the piazza. Lidi would do a few tricks and promise more amazing ones at the show that evening—for which, she made clear, tickets had to be bought. Later, Jericho pitched the tent in the nearest field. Sometimes a crowd came, sometimes not.

As for Daniella, Lidi and Jericho had become instantly devoted to her. The canvasmaster, for all his gruffness and grumbling, let the child ride on his shoulders, play with tent pegs, feed apples to the horses when there were any apples, and altogether doted on her. Lidi combed the girl's hair, primped and petted her as if Daniella were a little sister. Despite her past life in a burlap bag, Daniella was merry-hearted, quick to laugh. And had an appetite twice her size.

Only once did Lidi ask the child about her parents and how Zaccovelli had gotten hold of her. Daniella's lips tightened and she turned away.

"Your mother? Your father?" Lidi pressed on. Daniella did not answer. Lidi nodded. "I'd guess you're an orphan, then. Somebody without parents or family. Like me. No, that's not true," she quickly added. "I have a family. The best. Jericho."

"I have a family, too," Daniella said.

"Oh?" Lidi said. "You do?"

"Yes. Yours."

Until now, Daniella had been happy to do small chores, tidying the property wagon, fetching water, not getting underfoot during performances. One day, tagging after Lidi and hanging on her like a small barnacle, Daniella asked:

"When do I start my work?"

"You're working already," Lidi answered. "You want more to do? All right, you can help me lay out my costumes."

Daniella gave her the glance a seven-year-old gives to someone who has just spouted something outrageously ridiculous.

"That's not my work." She spoke kindly, patiently explaining the obvious to a slack-witted elder. "That's not what I'm supposed to do."

"It's plenty," Lidi said.

That particular afternoon, they pulled up by the fountain in the market square. Jericho strode back and forth, juggling flaming torches. His stomach was not in a mood to swallow any swords. Besides, the torches were a way of keeping the onlookers at a distance so Lidi had room to work. She had set up a folding table and draped a black cloth over it. She began some sleights with her cards, then abruptly stopped.

"It's later than I thought," she said. "What time is it? Who has a watch?"

With much laughter and joshing from his friends, a jolly-looking fellow let himself be nudged forward. Half-bashful, half-eager, but all in all happy to be the center of attention, he fished a gold watch from his breeches pocket. Lidi had found her mark.

"With your permission . . ." Lidi stepped toward him. Permission or not, she took the watch from his hand. "A splendid timepiece," she said. "But I think it needs a little adjustment. The mainspring could be overwound."

She went back to her table. She produced a sheet of paper and crinkled it around the watch. Her volunteer, who might have been having second thoughts, fidgeted. "Don't worry," she said, "just keep your eye on it."

On the table, the shape of the watch was clearly visible. The man seemed reassured.

"It's ticking too fast," Lidi said. "Listen. You can hear it for yourself. I'll fix it for you."

Among the cups and cards on her table lay a wooden mallet. Even though it took some effort for her to lift it, she swung it down with all her strength. There was a sickening crunch of delicate watchworks being squashed flat. The volunteer was too dumbstruck to blurt a protest. He opened and shut his mouth a few times. The best he could come out with was:

"I think you broke my watch."

"Oh. Sorry. Maybe I hit it too hard. Let's have a look."

Cautiously, she took away the crushed paper. Underneath it, nothing.

"Where did it go?" She glanced around. "Are you sure you gave me the watch in the first place?"

His friends burst out laughing, the volunteer's face turned pasty pale. Lidi strolled over to him.

"No, you couldn't have." She reached into his jacket. "Because . . . here it is."

Lidi produced the undamaged watch and returned it to its owner, whose fingers shook so much he could barely hold it. The onlookers whooped and clapped their hands.

It was a good effect. Lidi had done it well. The crinkled paper had convincingly shown its outline, but the watch itself was long gone. In a quick, smooth motion of her hand, she had whisked it into a secret pocket of her cloak. As for the heavy mallet, she could have picked it up with two fingers. Its head was light and hollow, with a few bits of scrap metal and broken glass inside. It was simple enough to palm the watch and make a show of finding it in the distressed owner's jacket.

About to do another effect, Lidi hesitated. She had an instinct about her audiences as a cat knows when someone plans to throw something at it. She knew when they were with her. She knew when she was losing them. Now she was losing them. Some stared past her, some drifted away. Jericho snuffed out his torches. He caught Lidi's eye and made a quick sweep of his hand across his throat. The signal warned her to close down and leave. She scooped up her equipment and folded the table.

A knot of townspeople, with more joining by the minute, had gathered at the rear of the property wagon. Jericho shouldered them aside. Lidi hurried in his wake.

5

The Added Attraction

DANIELLA SAT ON THE STEPS of the property wagon. She had one of Lidi's capes around her shoulders. As, one by one, the townsfolk approached, she leaned forward and spoke to each in turn. From the way they came up to her, she could have been a queen granting favors. Some of them kissed her hands.

Lidi went straight to her. She tried to be stern, which she could never be with Daniella. "I told you to stay in the wagon. What do you think you're doing?"

"Nothing." Daniella smiled blandly. "They ask me things. I answer."

"Who put you up to this, you imp?"

"Nobody," Daniella said. "I was just sitting here. They started coming—"

"Naturally." Lidi had no chance to hustle Daniella inside. The onlookers shouted indignantly. Angry protests and groans of disappointment welled up from the crowd as Jericho herded them clear of the wagon. Alarmed at first, he now could barely keep from doubling over with laughter.

"She's gone into business for herself," Jericho said out of the corner of his mouth.

"Worse," Lidi said. "She upstaged me."

"Make the best of it, Princess." Jericho chuckled. "And make the most of it. That's popular demand if I've ever seen it. You want my opinion? Tell them she'll appear again tonight. If you don't, they'll be disappointed. So disappointed they just might decide to eat you alive."

Lidi saw she had no choice. The child had caught her by surprise; she had to admire her for it, and even love her for it. But the crowd was turning restless, which was a step away from turning ugly. She did as Jericho said. She announced Daniella's return engagement. The onlookers cheered. Daniella wiggled her fingers at them.

Lidi boosted the child onto the driver's bench and slapped the reins. Jericho was already on his way to the field where they would pitch the tent.

"All right," Lidi said as Daniella beamed proudly, "what were you telling them back there?"

"Whatever came to me," Daniella said. "Sometimes, if I didn't see anything, I told the same thing over again."

"What was it?"

"Like this." Daniella closed her eyes and piped up in a play-song voice:

"Money will come into your hands. You'll go far and rise high."

"It fits everybody one way or another," Lidi said. "Even a wandering pickpocket, especially if he gets caught and hanged. For someone who used to live in a bag," she added, with a grin at Daniella, "you have the mind of a carnival faker—that's a compliment, in our line of business.

"But you need to learn," she went on. "You didn't control your audience enough. If you aren't in charge every minute, they can get out of hand, and that's as dangerous as a tent catching fire. So, no performing unless I'm with you. Or Jericho."

As they jogged along, a thought half playful, half serious, came to Lidi. "You've been telling other people's fortunes. What about mine? What do you see happening to me?"

"Money will come into your hands," Daniella said. "You'll go far and rise high—"

"Why, you little faker!" Lidi said in mock reproach. "I ask you something important and you fob me off with secondhand nonsense. Really, for an added attraction, you could have come up with a better prediction. At least one you haven't used."

"I answered you," Daniella said.

———————

Jericho was at the tent wagon when Lidi reined up. Leaving Daniella on the driver's bench, she helped him haul out the rolls of canvas.

"I'll get some paint when I'm done here," he said.

"What for?"

"I'll need to add a name on the side of the wagons. For the little one, if you want her to have her own act."

"I want?" Lidi said. "*She* wants. She's set on it. Can you see me telling her no? What do we call her? Something like—'Child of Destiny'? Or 'The Delightful—something or other'?"

"Keep it short," Jericho said. "I don't have a lot of paint."

"All right, then. Call her 'The Divine Daniella' . . . "

Daniella herself bounced up to Lidi and Jericho, as if she had a sixth sense for knowing when anyone was talking about her. She pranced up and down, Lidi's cape trailing behind her.

"Yes, that's what I'll be," she declared. She halted in mid-prance. "Oh—something more."

"What more?" said Lidi. "Enough is enough. You're too small for anything bigger."

"You need to say 'Added Attraction.'"

"Do it," Lidi said to Jericho.

Delighted with herself, Daniella crowed triumphantly. "I told you I was the Added Attraction. Didn't I? I told you so, I told you so."

"Don't remind me," Lidi said.

————

Jericho, who rarely admitted being satisfied with anything, was satisfied. "I think we'll have a straw house," he said.

"Where's the straw?" said Daniella.

"There isn't any," Lidi said. "That's what they call it in the circus. So many people come, they have to sit on piles of straw instead of seats." Lidi had no straw, and for benches, only some boards. Half the customers would have to stand. It would be her biggest crowd since she had come to Campania.

Lidi and Jericho had pitched the tent and hung lanterns all around. They rolled the tent wagon into the middle and let down one side of it to make a platform. At the rear, where no one would notice, was a narrow opening Lidi could use when she did vanishing acts. The property wagon stood just beyond, in what Jericho called the "backyard."

Daniella, as ordered, stayed out of sight behind a black backdrop. Jericho collected money at the entrance. It would be, as he said, a straw house. Latecomers had to be squeezed in. When there was no room even for one more body, Lidi began with "Hands of Glory," always a favorite. With her marvelous hands blazing away, she traced circles and spirals in the air. She brought out gleaming silver hoops that melted into one another to make a chain of glittering links. From nowhere, she produced endless strings of colored scarves and turned them into bouquets of silk flowers. And she smiled.

Without an assistant, she could not do her best illusions: "The Condemned Prisoner" and "The Basket of Swords." But the audience was high-spirited, quick to applaud, as good as she could have hoped. She also sensed a lot of them had come to see the child. After a last flourish of cards tumbling through the air like a waterfall, she announced that the added attraction, the Divine Daniella, had graciously consented to appear. She did not forget to mention the modest extra admission fee.

Jericho had lashed together some canvas panels and set up a narrow, open-fronted shelter. Lidi took Daniella through the backyard and into this makeshift pavilion. Jericho patrolled the entrance, collecting money and keeping the line of customers in order. Daniella sat at Lidi's folding table. Candles burned on either side. The child had taken permanent possession of Lidi's old cape and was close to being lost in its folds no matter how Lidi had pinned it up.

Lidi hovered nearby. The Divine Daniella was bright and lively, her face shone, she was more than ever pleased with herself. A long line of townspeople waited outside the pavilion. Lidi could not always hear what she whispered as each one came to the table. By now, it was close to midnight. A fine film of perspiration glistened on her forehead. Lidi watched her, troubled, as she told an old woman with a shawl over her head:

"Money will come into your hands. You'll go far and rise high."

This was the third time Daniella had made the same pronouncement. Lidi understood the child was at a loss for anything different to say. Her eyes were puffy, her shoulders sagged under the cape. The old woman, as far as Lidi could see, was the last in line. She signaled Jericho that she was closing down the performance.

Lidi was about to pick up the child and carry her to the

property wagon. A man in a dark suit had weaseled his way into the tent, dodging and twisting out of Jericho's grasp until the canvasmaster finally got hold of him by the coattails.

"Let her speak to me. She must!" He strained closer to the table. "The hours I waited? I won't be denied—"

"Come back tomorrow," Lidi said.

"Don't tell me tomorrow. Now. Time is money. I must be served." The man pointed a beaky nose at Daniella, who yawned at him. "I demand it."

"Demand nothing," Lidi said. "The show's over. Go away."

"You don't know who you're dealing with." In spite of Jericho's grip on his coat, he drew himself up with as much authority as he could muster in the circumstances. "Scabbia. That name means nothing to you? Ask anyone. They all know Scabbia. I am not a man who is told to go away."

"I just did that." Lidi looked him up and down. He wore a pinch-waisted, bottle-green suit, outdated even for the provinces. She wondered if he had bought it secondhand.

"Scabbia," he repeated. "Mortgage holder. Money-lender—"

"Don't feel too bad about it," Lidi said. "You could have been a lawyer."

"Important business, delicate negotiations. I must know the outcome, how to conduct myself." He dipped his fingers into his waistcoat. "Here. I pay double what you ask."

He blustered on about his transactions, profits to be made, wealth to be won. When he saw Lidi was deeply unimpressed, he changed over to whining and pleading.

Without a prediction from the Divine Daniella, he would be ruined, made to starve on the streets. He wrung his hands, clutched his chest. He looked ready to fling himself to his knees, or if it came to that, roll on the ground.

Lidi's patience was already frayed. It was Daniella who settled the matter. She nodded and waved him closer. Lidi saw a thread of a smile on her lips.

"Money will come into your hands." Daniella spoke slowly and carefully. *"You will go far and rise high."*

"Ah." Scabbia brightened. He ran his tongue around his teeth, sucking the marrow out of her words. "Ah. Yes. That's good. Tell more."

Daniella shut her eyes and turned away. Lidi motioned for Scabbia to go. "That's all."

"Of course. I understand. Another time, another fee." Scabbia kissed his fingertips. He grinned like a blissful ferret as Jericho prodded him out of the tent.

"What a little imp you are," Lidi said.

"I'll sleep now," Daniella said.

6

Julian

THERE WAS NO STRAW HOUSE the next night; the night after that, barely a house at all, only a handful of an audience. Even the line of townsfolk waiting for the Divine Daniella dwindled to half a dozen.

"You did well. It's not your fault," Jericho told Lidi later, when she tucked the child in bed. Lidi had reclaimed the cot and made a kind of nest for Daniella with blankets and old costumes behind the curtain of the property wagon. "Most all the town came the first night. Now they've seen the show, they won't pay to see the same thing again."

"Daniella handled herself better than I expected," Lidi said. "She'll be fine. But you're right, I'll have to think of something new for each performance. Until I find Ferramondo."

"Still set on that rope trick?" Jericho asked. "Still the wild-goose chase?"

"Can you think of a better one?" Lidi answered.

Next morning, Jericho began striking the tents. Daniella was still asleep. Lidi went toward the property wagon to wake her up and give her breakfast.

A horse and light carriage rattled across the field. Lidi groaned. She felt as if burrs had gotten tangled in her hair.

Scabbia was driving as fast as the horse could trot.

She ran to wave him away. Scabbia reined up. "We're closed," she said. "Don't bother to get down."

Scabbia got down anyway. He was not wearing the bottle-green suit but a better-quality black coat and tight trousers. On him, they still looked shabby. He stepped closer to Lidi, who was doing her best to escape, and plucked her by the sleeve.

"How much do you want for her?"

Lidi stared at him. "What are you talking about?"

"The child." Scabbia twitched impatiently. "The child. What price?"

Lidi had trouble believing what she was hearing. She had, at first, taken him for an infuriating nuisance. She decided he was an infuriating lunatic.

"There isn't a price. Nobody's for sale."

"There's always a price. Everything has a price."

"Not everything." Lidi turned away. Scabbia kept after

her, nearly treading on her heels. The more she tried to shake him off, the more he clutched at her, a persistent skin rash.

"Won't sell? Oh, yes, I see you're a shrewd one." Scabbia managed to step in front of her. "All right, you don't want to sell. Will you rent?

"Listen, I'll rent her from you," he pressed. "A lease, like real estate. You'll have a share in the profits. Nice business for you.

"I need her." Scabbia was twisting around like a corkscrew. "She can tell me what to do—"

"I could tell you what to do," Lidi said.

"You don't understand. *It happened.*"

Scabbia was not a man to give anything away; certainly not money, certainly not valuable information. In this case, he could not keep it to himself. It was too big, too astonishing. He was bursting with it. And he wanted the child.

"It came true, don't you see?" he whispered. "True as she told me. Money will come into my hands. It did.

"I was going to my countinghouse. I turned into a backstreet, and there it was, in a corner against the wall, lying in a heap of rubbish. A purse full of money. Just waiting to be picked up. For *me* to pick up.

"There has to be more to come," he hurried on. "She knows. She knows secret things. She'll tell me what to buy and sell, the best investments for the biggest profits. There's a fortune in her—"

"I've heard enough out of you," Lidi said. "Just be glad

for your luck. The same could have happened to anybody."

"No. It was foretold to me. It was promised."

"Do you want to talk to Jericho about it?"

Scabbia hesitated. His eyes were hard and bright. He walked to his carriage. Before he climbed aboard, he gave Lidi a yellow smile.

"I get what I want," he said.

She watched until the carriage was out of sight. She went toward the property wagon. Jericho, finished with the tents, came up to her.

"That weasel Scabbia was back," Lidi began. "I sent him away. He makes my skin crawl. You can't imagine what he wanted . . ." Then she noticed a young man following a couple of paces behind Jericho. "Who's that?"

"His name's Julian. So he tells me," Jericho said. "I found him hiding under the tent wagon."

"Hiding from what?" Lidi said.

The newcomer stepped beside Jericho. He was as tall as the canvasmaster, but rawboned and lankier. He wore a scuffed leather vest, coarse cotton trousers, heavy-soled clogs; not the typical garb in this province.

"I wasn't hiding," he said. "I was sleeping."

"You were sleeping while you were hiding," Jericho said to him. And, to Lidi: "What else he's been doing, sneaking around—"

The young man's chin went up. "I'm not a thief."

"Who said you were?" Lidi put in.

"I doubt that he's a thief," Jericho said. "Catch a thief,

the first thing he does is yelp and carry on and swear it was two other people. This fellow claims he's looking for work.

"I'll give him this much," Jericho added. "He seems willing enough. He helped me stow the tents. I didn't ask. He offered. He didn't even talk about money."

"I'm glad he didn't," Lidi said. "What do you think?"

"Well, my sense of it," Jericho said, "he's no worse than your usual roustabout. He's got a strong back, a good pair of arms. He doesn't look altogether stupid, which is an extra benefit."

"You could use the help," Lidi said. "For that matter, so could I. He's too big for 'The Basket of Swords.' He might do for 'The Condemned Prisoner.'"

"You talk as if I were a horse," Julian said. "Do you want to look at my teeth?"

"Not especially," Lidi told him. "We're only trying to decide what to do."

She studied him for a few moments. He waited, hands on hips, studying her likewise. His hair was ragged at the ends, as if he had trimmed it with a dull saw. His lean, sun-scorched face was full of hungry hollows. He did not look as if he made a habit of eating. There was, even so, something challenging in his bearing. Jericho had made a rare misjudgment. This was not the usual roustabout.

She smelled the fear, then, the way an animal smells fear. No more than a faint wisp, but it was there. She seemed to glimpse a ghost flickering behind his eyes. A painful ghost.

She felt it in her heart. She did not want him to have such a ghost. What she wanted was to touch his face.

"It would be good," Jericho was saying, "to stir up some noise when we go into town. A bass drum. Or a trombone. Can you play a trombone?" he said to Julian. "Not that it matters. We don't have a trombone."

"You know the work we do," Lidi said.

Julian shook his head. "Some kind of show."

"You haven't seen it?"

"No. I've only been here since last night."

"A magic show," Lidi said. "You know what they're like."

"They never came to my town."

"Which is where?"

Julian made a vague gesture. "Another province."

"You're not a fountain of information," Lidi said. "You worked at something?"

"I was a *cafone*," Julian said. "A tenant farmer. We get paid for a share of our crops."

"With us, you won't get paid at all. Maybe later," Lidi said. "Food—you'll eat what we have. When we have it. Agreed?"

"So far, yes."

"We'll take you on, then." She had already made up her mind about that. She had made it up from the first moment.

"I'll fix a place for you in the tent wagon," Jericho said. "Now, my lad, you're a first-of-May."

"That's what we call newcomers," Lidi said. "They show up when the weather gets warm. When it turns cold, they leave." After a moment, she added, "Is that what you'll do?"

He did not answer. Daniella came out of the property wagon. She rubbed sleep from her eyes.

"This is Julian," Lidi said. "He'll be working with us now."

"I'm the Added Attraction," Daniella said to him. She turned to Lidi. "Will he be our family, too?"

"That depends," Lidi said, "on what he wants."

"He wants breakfast," Daniella said. "So do I."

"Later," Lidi said. "I need to be away from here. This place turns my stomach. Scabbia came back again."

"I knew he would," Daniella said.

The canvasmaster motioned for Julian to follow him. They stopped at the tent wagon.

"Two kinds of people I'd rather stay clear of," Jericho said. "Troublemakers and trouble magnets. The ones who start trouble and the ones who attract it. I don't know which you are."

He laid a hand on Julian's arm. "Let's be frank. You're on the shady side of the law; it sticks out all over you. Not that I hold it against anyone—no, don't lie, you're not old enough to be a good liar. You're just a first-of-May, so you keep your mouth shut and do as you're told.

"That doesn't suit you?" Jericho added as Julian bristled.

"I don't need to be told how to work. Or keep my mouth shut."

"Well, here you do. This is a magic show, not a tomato patch. Another thing. The princess. With her, you'll mind your own business." Jericho had actually taken half a liking to him, so he said as pleasantly as he could, "Or I'll disconnect you joint by joint."

"You might try." Julian grinned at him.

"We'd find out, wouldn't we?" Jericho tightened his fingers. "But you take my meaning. Oh, yes, my lad, I saw that look."

"What look?" Julian said. "What about my look?"

"Not yours," Jericho said. "Hers."

7

The First-of-May

TWO MOUNTED OFFICERS OF the *carabinieri* came just after breakfast. Daniella was the first to see them as they galloped around the bend of the road. She waved at them.

"Nice horsies," she said.

The officers pulled up at the roadside and swung down from their saddles. They wore uniforms of close-fitting, brass-buttoned jackets with white cross straps, military breeches, and black cocked hats. They carried small, short-barreled muskets slung over their shoulders like ugly toys.

Lidi was sitting by the cook fire. She got up and went to them, holding back Daniella, who tried to go and pat the horsies.

"Something you want?" she said.

One of the officers had sun-reddened cheeks. A rusty mustache sprawled across most of his face. He was a sergeant, with stripes like white sardines on his sleeve. He saluted stiffly. He was brisk but not impolite.

"You're to come with us, signorina."

"Why should I do that?" Lidi said.

Jericho had come to her side. The sergeant found him larger than expected. He saluted again. Julian, as a first-of-May, had been given the job of washing up. He still had the tin plates and pans in his hands. When he saw the *carabinieri,* he took a few steps back and watched from the shadow of the property wagon.

"There's a charge laid against *la maga* Lidi—the magician girl. That's you," the sergeant said. "You have to answer to the tribunal."

"Charge of what?" Lidi said.

"A criminal complaint." From his jacket the *carabiniere* took a square of paper and unfolded it. The document was covered with official seals, stamps, and endorsements enough to intimidate the most innocent, which was mainly the point of it.

"Theft," he said. "A large sum of cash."

"Ridiculous," Lidi said. "We're not thieves."

"Then you'll have no trouble proving your case, will you?" the sergeant said. "But the accusation has been made."

"Who made it?" Lidi said. She already knew.

"Signor Scabbia—"

"Yes. Well, he's a liar."

"A respected citizen, signorina. A gentleman of distinction."

"Distinguished for what?" Lidi said. "For being a notorious weasel?"

"Crocodile," the other *carabiniere* put in helpfully. He was a corporal, a younger man, country-bred, who had joined for the sake of the uniform. "Crocodile is what they call him, the people who owe him money."

"You get a first hearing before the examining magistrate," the sergeant went on. "Then the presiding judge. Before that, the depositions, verifications, and so on. If things move along quickly, you'll only have to wait maybe six months.

"Until your case is tried, you'll be locked up, of course. Don't worry. If you're guilty, you'll get credit for time served. If you're innocent, you'll get deepest apologies. So, consider yourself under arrest. All of you."

"And the child?"

"And the child."

"As I expected," Lidi said.

"The warrant's for three people." The corporal had been admiring the painted wagons. He jerked his head at Julian. "There's four."

"So there is," the sergeant said. "I'll see about that." He strode up to Julian, who looked squarely at him, jaws tight and muscles tense.

"He works for me," Lidi said. "He has nothing to do with any of this."

"Doesn't matter," the sergeant said. "All fish in the same net. He's under arrest, too."

Julian threw his handful of tinware in the *carabiniere*'s face.

The man flinched and stumbled back. He had never been attacked by someone he was supposed to arrest. Before he could think about what was happening, Julian sprang at him and wrestled him to the ground.

"Fool!" Jericho shouted. "What are you doing?"

The younger officer stared for a moment. He unslung his musket and ran to help his superior. Daniella wrapped her arms around his legs and hung on. The corporal went sprawling. Lidi snatched the musket.

Julian had his knee on the sergeant's chest. He gripped the man's throat with one hand and tore at his cross straps with the other. The unhappy *carabiniere* was too entangled in his own gear to do more than flop around uselessly. His cocked hat had bounced away.

"Get rope," Julian called. "Tie them up."

"Do it," Lidi told Jericho. Things had gotten too far out of hand; she saw no other choice. The canvasmaster, endlessly cursing Julian, did as she said. The situation was insane. He resigned himself to acting like a madman.

"Take the uniforms." Julian ripped at the sergeant's brass buttons. "Take the guns. The horses."

"Just take it all. Why not?" Jericho said through his teeth. "The fat's in the fire now, you lunatic."

"I'd be willing to forget any of this happened," the sergeant said.

"So would I." Lidi kept the musket aimed at the younger *carabiniere*.

"You're not going to hurt us, are you?" he said.

"I'd rather not."

"I saw your show," he said. "It was very good. I liked it."

"I'm glad," Lidi said. "Take off your boots."

Daniella observed these doings with interest. Julian slung both muskets over his shoulder. Lidi bundled up the uniforms and the rest of the gear. Julian ran to the horses. He swung astride one and took the reins of the other.

"This way," he called. He trotted the horses toward the woodland and waved for Lidi and Jericho to follow.

"Let him go," Jericho said. "Be done with him. He's put us in enough of a mess."

"Is there another way out of it?" Lidi tossed the bundle into the property wagon and sent Daniella along with it. She climbed to the driver's bench and slapped the reins. Jericho, shaking his head, got aboard the tent wagon.

The draft horses with their heavy loads could not keep up with the *carabinieri*'s mounts. Julian slowed his gait so Lidi would not lose sight of him. The wagons lurched across the broken ground. Once, they nearly tipped over. Within another hour, they came into a grove of chestnut trees. There it was cooler, the earth soft and grassy. Lidi pulled up to rest the winded horses. Daniella popped out of the wagon.

"Are we eating again?" she said.

Jericho, still muttering, examined the wheels and axles. Finding no serious damage, he gave his full attention to Julian, who had tethered the stolen horses to a fallen limb.

"What kind of idiot are you? What have you done to us?"

Jericho looked an inch from laying hands on the younger man. "We're in for it now."

"You were in for it already." Julian stood eye to eye with the canvasmaster. "Or do you like the idea of rotting in jail?"

"I don't like the idea of the law on my heels," Jericho said. "When those two get themselves loose and go back to town, what happens then? Whatever else, now we're horse thieves. I don't feel called upon to thank you for that."

"Let him be," Lidi said. "He's right. We'd be rotting in jail. Waiting to be tried? How long? Answer charges? It's Scabbia's word against ours. He knows exactly what he's doing. He doesn't care about us. Daniella's the one he's after. With us locked up, that's his best chance at her."

Jericho rubbed his sweating face. "All right, we were caught in a trap. Damned if we do, damned if we don't. I still don't like it."

"You were quick off the mark back there," said Lidi, her eyes on Julian. "You've had some practice. You do that sort of thing a lot?"

"Not if I can help it."

"You didn't know why they were after us," Lidi said. "Were you helping us—or yourself?"

"Nobody wants trouble with the law," Julian said.

"Some have better reasons than others," Jericho said. Then he added, "You need to change your clothes. You've been seen, they won't forget you. You can't go around in that outfit. May as well wear a sign on your back: 'Arrest me.' I'll find something."

"We've been seen, too," Lidi said. "And not forgotten."

Jericho went to rummage in the tent wagon. Daniella sidled closer to Julian. She smiled sweetly at him. As a child, in all innocent affection, asks a bald man where his hair went, she said:

"Why do you have blood on your hands?"

8

The Cafone

"HUSH." LIDI PUT A FINGER to Daniella's lips. "You're being silly."

"I'm not," Daniella said.

"Go pat the horsies," Lidi told her.

The child skipped off. Julian abruptly turned away. He went to sit on the steps of the property wagon, his long legs drawn up and his elbows on his knees. He was staring at his palms.

"Pay no attention." Lidi sat beside him. She took one of his hands. "There's no blood."

"She saw it. She said it."

"She's likely to say anything. You never know what she'll

come out with next. I don't think she does, either. She didn't mean anything by it."

Julian's face darkened. There had been, with the *carabinieri,* a moment when Lidi had seen a blaze in his eyes that frightened her. Now something was hurting him. She saw herself putting her arms around him; and so she might have done, but here was Jericho with some old clothes.

"Make do with these." The canvasmaster tossed Julian a faded blue jacket, patched trousers, and a shirt. "The horses— you can ride one and lead the other. Those are military saddles, so get rid of them. The muskets and cartridge boxes—if you take them, bundle them up. You don't want to be seen carrying firearms, do you? Food—I'll pack what we can spare."

"Why are you telling him this?" Lidi said.

"Considering that little scuffle this morning," Jericho said, "you know as well as I do he's on the run." He gave a dour smile. "And so are we, now. I assumed we'd part company, good-bye, no hard feelings, and go our own ways."

"I didn't assume that," Lidi said. She turned to Julian. "Is that what you want?"

"If that's what you want," he said.

"You'd be safer with us," Lidi said. "For the time being, anyhow. You can stay out of sight in the tent wagon. If we can stay out of sight ourselves. With 'Princess Lidi' and the 'Divine Daniella' all over everything, we'd be hard to miss."

"I don't have paint enough to cover the lettering," Jericho said. "Plaster it with mud? That won't answer too well. Not after the first rainstorm."

"You don't need to do that," Julian said. "It's simple. Cross over to another province. Alto-Trento's the nearest. Those were local *carabinieri*. They won't go past the border. Once you're away from here, nobody will bother to look twice at you."

"How do we get across?" Lidi said. "What about guard posts? Tollhouses? We've been stopped and had to pay toll at each one since we came here."

"Do what everyone else does," Julian said. "Take a smugglers' trail. There are more of them than there are roads; some of them better paved."

"We're already horse thieves, we may as well be smugglers," Jericho said. "Just as a matter of curiosity, what do people around here have to smuggle?"

"Nothing the next province doesn't have. Wine, sausage, cheese—the same things back and forth. They taste better when they're smuggled."

"This is a crazy country," Jericho said.

"Very crazy," Julian said. "Also, very beautiful. You have to understand: It's a sort of game. It makes our masters look foolish. It makes us feel like human beings. It's worth the risk."

"Do we have a better choice?" Lidi said. "We can't let ourselves be caught again."

"No, we'll have to do it," Jericho said, after a moment. "We'll move out when it's dark. But I can tell you I'm not fond of driving rattletrap wagons along some godforsaken trail at night."

"You won't drive at night," Julian said. "It's too crowded then. That's when most of the smugglers are out. And the *carabinieri*. Before sundown, there's hardly anybody. I know a good path."

"For someone who's not from around here, you know a lot," Lidi said.

"I learn quickly," Julian said.

"Another matter of curiosity," the canvasmaster said. "You didn't get off to a good start with us. I won't claim it's all your fault. But I'd sleep easier if I knew who we're dealing with.

"I'm satisfied you're not a thief," he went on. "That leaves some other interesting possibilities. It's true if every first-of-May had to be a choirboy there wouldn't be enough to go 'round. So, in our line of work, we don't look too closely."

"Then let him be," Lidi said. "It's none of our business."

"Maybe so, maybe not." The canvasmaster held his eyes on Julian. "Only answer me this: How much is it worth?"

"What's worth?"

"Your head. You won't sit there, my lad, and try to tell me there isn't a price on it."

Julian stiffened. "Suppose there is. What difference does it make?"

"A lot. If someone's looking to do you in and collect a reward for it, and we just happen to be standing inconveniently in the way—that's a little detail we ought to know about. You appreciate my concern."

"As long as I stay out of Ardita Vecchia—"

"What's that, yet another province?" Jericho said. "This country has more of them than the world has miseries."

"I can't go there," Julian said. "If I do, I'm probably dead. Does that satisfy your curiosity?"

"Good reason to stay away. I can't think of a better," Jericho said. "A fellow like you can get himself in trouble anywhere. Why that place more than another?"

"You have to understand the Ardita," Julian said. "It has the richest soil in Campania. Everything grows there. Grain, fruit, olives, grapes. We have a saying: Put a stick in the ground, next day you have a fig tree. It's wonderful. One trouble: The people who do the growing also do most of the starving."

"That doesn't make sense," Lidi said.

"Did you expect sense?" Jericho said. "It's a crazy country. He admits it himself."

"I was born there," Julian said. "I grew up on the Marchese di Malvento's estate. One of the *latifundia*—the big landholdings, so big you can't walk across them in a day. The Villa Malvento—the mansion house, outbuildings, a private park. Small compared with some others."

"A sweet life for the Marchese di Whatever," Jericho said.

"Him? No," Julian said. "The landlords don't live on their estates. Some don't even live in Campania. Nobody's seen him, not ever. For all I know, he's not a real *marchese*. The old noble families are happy to sell off a few of their titles when they're pinched for cash. Enough money, you can buy the right to call yourself *marchese,* or duke, or prince, with the family crest thrown in for good measure.

"The *cafoni* work the land and raise the crops," Julian went on. "We pay a share of all we grow. The *padrone,* the overseer, makes sure we do. He squeezes us for every bushel he can get. A good harvest, we pay extra; a bad harvest, we pay to make up for the loss."

"That's not fair," Lidi broke in. "Nobody comes out against him?"

"No," Julian said. "He's the real lord of the manor. He does what he pleases, there's no law but what he says it is. He might as well be king of his own private kingdom.

"Our *padrone* was named Babbo. We called him 'the Baboon.' A big man with a big face. He looked as if he had a side of beef under his coat.

"If I see him again," Julian said, "I'll kill him."

9

The Baboon

"ON THE OTHER HAND, YOU NEVER KNOW how these things work out," Julian said. "He might end up killing me. He'd very much like to do that."

"Not bosom friends," Lidi said.

"With a *padrone*?" Julian made a wry face. "Better off being friends with a hyena."

"They're all that bad?" Lidi said.

"All? I don't know. I never met a hyena, I don't mean to insult an honest animal. I only know the Baboon."

"What about him, then?" Lidi said. "No, never mind," she added, seeing the ghost come flickering back into Julian's eyes. "It's not my business."

"That's right. Not your business. Not the parts I don't

like; especially the parts I don't like. But if that's what you want—I owe you that much."

"You owe me nothing."

"I do. A matter of principle.

"One afternoon," he went on, "my uncle Renzo and I drove a cartload of grain to the weighing shed. Renzo—he and his wife raised me after my parents died. That's how we do things in Campania. We keep it in the family. The family's the *cafone*'s kingdom. So, Renzo was helping me haul the grain.

"The way it works," Julian said, "they tally what we bring. The Baboon marks it down to our account. Less what we borrowed against the harvest. We always borrow against the harvest.

"The Baboon cheats. We know. He doesn't fool us. The scales are a little off, so are the totals. We don't get full credit on the account books.

"He keeps the difference for himself. Then he skims a bit from what he hands over to the estate agent, who skims a bit more when he sends it to the *marchese*. We're used to that. We expect rats to nibble.

"But the Baboon was getting greedy. He was going a long way past nibbling. We couldn't wink at it, he was rubbing our noses in it. Cheat us a little, *va bene,* let it go. Cheat us too much—it insults our intelligence.

"We have to draw the line somewhere," Julian added. "Another matter of principle."

"You seem to have a lot of them," Lidi said.

"Some," Julian said. "Everything else costs too much."

"I always found having principles costs too much," Jericho said. "I can only afford a few."

"It comes to the same." Julian shrugged and went on.

"The Baboon sits at his table in the shed, with his ledgers and cashbooks, his chums lounging around. After it's all weighed, and counted, and noted down, he looks up at me. He has a funny grin on his face.

"'Well, boy,' he says, 'all calculations done, it comes to the grand sum total'—he runs a finger down the column of numbers—'yes, what I see here is: zero. You understand zero? *Niente*. Nothing. So, that's what you get.'

"I had made up my mind I wouldn't swallow any more of his robbery. I told him no, he's wrong, he made a mistake.

"'What mistake? Who makes a mistake?' He turns to his chums. They were laughing and nudging each other. 'Do we make mistakes here?'

"'Never, *padrone*,' says Muzio, one of his toadies.

"I told him I wanted the tally done over, and I wanted to see the accounts.

"The Baboon had started laughing, too. When he saw I meant it, he stopped.

"'Don't get smart with me. What, you're some kind of lawyer? You've got a big enough mouth for one. You want a fist in it?'

"Renzo was pulling my arm and telling me be quiet, be quiet. He had been a strong man in his day, but he was old now and they were too many for us. He wanted to go home.

"'Count again,' I said.

"The Baboon gets up and comes around the table. He

has a walking stick with a silver knob. He always carries it. He thinks it makes him look elegant, a *gentiluomo,* a real gentleman. He jams the knob under my chin and pushes my head back.

"'No. You count,' he says. 'You count yourself lucky I don't give you a beating.'

"I knocked the stick away. He swings it and catches me on the side of the head. Before he can do it again, I hit him in the face. His nose starts bleeding. The Baboon pulls out a handkerchief to mop it up. He chokes and spits.

"'You bastard,' he says. He tells Muzio and the others to get hold of me. I couldn't shake them off. Renzo was shouting at him. I think he'd have gone at the Baboon, but someone shoved him to the ground. A couple of them threw me over a barrel and hung on to my arms and legs. The Baboon rips away my shirt. He picks up a horsewhip from a corner of the shed.

"'I'll make you squeal for that,' he says. "You'll scream your head off before I'm done.'

"I swear to myself I won't give him that satisfaction, no matter what he does. A matter of principle, you understand. I tried to think of other things, to take my mind off what was happening. But the Baboon kept on; I lost track of what I was thinking about. I lost track of everything. I don't remember, but somebody must have helped Renzo throw me into the cart.

"When we get home, my aunt Bella cries and carries on when she sees me. She and Renzo put me facedown on a mattress. She goes to get rags and a bucket of water. I couldn't feel my back yet, but my mouth hurt. I must have bitten through my lips. Renzo was sitting beside me.

"'He didn't get what he wanted,' I said. 'He didn't get anything out of me.'

"'Not really,' Renzo said. 'Just at the end. Everybody breaks, sooner or later. You couldn't help it. It doesn't matter.'

"'To me it does.'

"That was when I decided I had to kill the Baboon. As soon as I felt better. Later, I knew it wasn't a good idea, it could make things worse for everybody. I'd do it somehow, but meantime I had a plan.

"When I was up and around, I told my friend Matteo and the other lads what I had in mind. They were all for it. The older men, not so much. Silence is the old man's weapon. I talked to Renzo. Everyone respected him; I wanted him to be with us.

"We'd go, I told him, six or eight of us, face-to-face with the Baboon. From now on, we'd be the ones to make sure the scales were honest; and we'd see all the account books. If the Baboon didn't agree, I knew what we could do.

"At first, Renzo wanted no part of it. He only saw trouble. We talked more, it took a while until I got him to change his mind. I promised him we could make it work.

"A few days after that, we all went to the weighing shed. Matteo wanted us to carry pitchforks and rakes. I told him no. If the Baboon thought we were looking for a fight, he'd only dig his heels in.

"He was surprised to see us, and not happy about it. 'You

again?' he said to me. 'You didn't get enough last time? You're back for more?'

"'A lot more,' I said.

"'I should have known you were behind all this,' he said, after I told him what we demanded. He stayed calmer than I expected. He only cursed at us until he ran out of breath, then looked at us as if we were a bunch of stupid children. He ordered us to clear out and mind our own business. I had our answer for him.

"'There won't be any business,' I said. 'We plant nothing, we grow nothing, we harvest nothing.'

"'Now there's a clever *cafone* for you,' he says to his chums hanging around the shed. 'He'll cut off his nose to spite his face.' Then, to us: 'You'll hurt yourselves more than you'll ever hurt me. My belly won't be empty. Yours will.'

"'We're used to that,' I said. 'But if we grow nothing, we share nothing with the estate. No crops, no profit for the *marchese*. And who's he going to blame? The *padrone*. You. I'll be surprised if he doesn't kick you out and get a new overseer. We'll still be here. You'll be gone.'

"This brought him up short. He chewed on his thumbnail awhile. His face got heavy.

"'I'm a reasonable man,' he said then. 'Good faith on both sides, we can all work this out. My word on it. I'll need a little time to get the details in order. Come here again in an hour. No, say an hour and a half. A bargain? *Bene.*'

"We went back to our houses. Houses—more like frame shanties in a cluster at the edge of the estate. Everybody came out to see what had happened. We all stood around on the hard-packed ground in front of the houses, our own sort of village square. You'd have thought it was a holiday. We knew the Baboon had been quick to agree, maybe too quick. We expected he'd find something to haggle over. Still, we believed he had sense enough, at the end, to give us what we asked. So we were in pretty good spirits, talking and joking, waiting for the time to go back to the weighing shed.

"We didn't go back. The Baboon came to us. Before the hour had gone by, he drove up in a wagon, his chums with him and a few men I didn't recognize, probably from the next estate. They had clubs and sticks, some of them carried muskets."

10

The Hunted

"I KNEW, THEN," JULIAN SAID. "He lied to us. He played us for fools. And I was the biggest fool of all, because I hadn't foreseen it. I didn't know what to do. If there was anything to do.

"They all jumped down from the wagon and walked over to where we were standing. I was in front of Renzo's house. My aunt Bella was in the doorway. Renzo was beside me, muttering about trouble. I told him to go inside. He wouldn't. The Baboon stops in front of me.

"'Smart, are you?' he shouts in my face. 'Think you get away with this?' He waves his stick. 'Threaten me? Intimidate me? You'll have something you didn't ask for.'

"He looks around at the others and changes his tone:

"'I know all you boys,' he says nicely. 'You're good fellows. Forget this nonsense. I'll let it go by, no hard feelings. It's not your fault. You listened to some hothead with a grudge against me. Blame him if you end up in a mess. He started this. He's the one I want. Be sensible, the rest of you, and this is over and done with.'

"The Baboon turns to me again. 'Step out, boy. Come quiet, maybe I go a little easier on you.'

"I heard Matteo call to me not to do it; the others hooted and shook their fists at the Baboon. I didn't move. I wonder now if I should have.

"'That's how it is?' the Baboon says. He puts his stick on the ground. He opens his coat and pulls a pistol from his belt.

"'Here's what it comes down to,' he says. 'Do as you're told or I shoot you where you stand, like the dog you are.'

"I thought he was bluffing, even when he cocked the pistol. All of us together, I was sure we could face him down. The Baboon had the pistol in both hands, pointing it at me. His finger twitched on the trigger.

"It happened fast. There was a big, cracking explosion. The same time the Baboon fired, Renzo jumped in front of me. The bullet hit him in the chest, he fell back in my arms. Everything went quiet. We all froze. Smoke from the muzzle hung in the air. I could hear the crows scolding in the woods beyond the houses.

"It all went crazy, then. The men with the muskets began shooting. Everybody scattered. I dragged Renzo into the house. Bella was crying and waving her arms; she kept saying why did we ever start this whole business. We laid him down on the floor and bundled some blankets under his head. Blood was all over his shirt. He kept gasping for breath. He turned his eyes on me. He couldn't speak. He looked sad and small.

"I didn't know what was happening outside. I only knew they'd be coming for me. I told Bella I had to get away.

"'No,' she said. 'We can hide you. Here or in other houses. A dozen different places.'

"I told her somebody was bound to talk. The Baboon would make them. Then it would be all the worse for everyone.

"'If I'm gone, I'm gone,' I said. 'He can't blame you for it.'

"Bella nodded. 'Do what you think best.'

"She kissed me on both cheeks. I went through the back door. I ran into the woods. I knew of a cave near a dry creek bed. I meant to hole up awhile. Maybe it would all blow over. I doubted that.

"At the end of the day, Matteo found me. He guessed where I'd be. We played there when we were boys. He told me things I didn't want to hear. Renzo was dead. The Baboon had the *carabinieri* hunting me. I was to be arrested and taken to the town tribunal. No question, I'd get a death sentence.

"They should arrest the Baboon, I told him. He was the one who shot Renzo. We saw him do it.

"'An old *cafone*?' Matteo says. 'Means nothing. You're who they want. Provocation, inciting to riot. They're going to make an example of you. Some of the estate agents got together and offered a reward. Big. Tempting, if anyone wants a pocketful of money. Get out of Ardita. As far as you can go.'

"'I want the Baboon,' I told him. 'Blood for blood.'

"'You'll never get him. Not if you're dead.'

"'You have a point,' I said.

"We talked some more. I understood he was right. We said good-bye then. I left during the night. I kept thinking about Renzo. He didn't want anything to do with this. I talked him into it. I had his blood on my hands as if I'd pulled the trigger myself.

"The rest of it," Julian said. "I got across the border. I kept moving. I stayed alive. That's all."

Lidi had been listening quietly, eyes on Julian. She said, "You can't go home."

"One day, yes," Julian said. "I have to. A matter of principle."

Lidi, for the first time, noticed Daniella eavesdropping. "Go play. You shouldn't hear these things."

"I don't mind," Daniella said. "It doesn't bother me. I used to live in a bag."

"A touching story." Jericho cocked an eye at him. "I'd be touched even more if you tell me this. Reward, you say? A big one? For a *cafone*? How is it you're such a valuable fellow?"

"I told you," Julian said. "They want to make an example. Like hanging dead crows in a cornfield. It scares away the others.

"So no one dares to try that again," he added. "What if somebody else did? And made it work. Then others do it. And it spreads all over Ardita. Maybe all over Campania."

"You're a walking infection, then," Jericho said. "Could be, I suppose. Just one thing more. Flogged, were you? Terrible ordeal, it must have been. Bound to leave some nasty marks. Take off your shirt, my lad. Let's have a look."

Julian stood up. "Go to the devil."

He turned on his heel and walked away.

"You shouldn't have asked that," Lidi said.

She went to find him. He was standing behind the tent wagon. He had stripped off his old shirt to put on the one Jericho had given him.

She saw his back, from shoulders to waist. It looked as if dogs had been at it.

He heard her footsteps. He did not turn to face her. "He didn't believe me. May as well as call me a liar. Do you want to see? Go on, take a good look."

She went closer. She touched her lips to the scars across his shoulders.

"Why did you do that?" Julian said.

"I do what I do."

"I do what I have to." Julian wheeled around. "I'm a first-of-May. You told me. They come when the weather gets warm. When it gets cold, they go."

"Not always."

She thought, for a moment, he was going to reach out to her.

"I need to put on my shirt," he said.

She left him there. Jericho was sitting on the steps of the property wagon.

"He told the truth," Lidi said. "I know. I saw."

"I had to be sure," Jericho said. "The world is full of liars."

"He's not one of them," Lidi said. "He's ashamed of himself."

"I'm sorry," Jericho said. "I'm ashamed of myself, too."

"Don't be."

She told him nothing more. It was the first time she had kept anything from him.

11

The Vanishing Coin

"I'M THINKING ABOUT HORSES," Jericho said.

"I think about them a lot," Daniella said.

Julian had found the smugglers' trail. It was hardly wide enough for the wagons, rutted, rocky, here and there over-grown with weeds.

"What the devil did you get us into?" Jericho burst out when the tent wagon lurched and nearly tipped over. "You told us it was a good path."

"If I told you it was a bad path, would you have taken it?" Julian said.

"Of course not," Jericho admitted.

Daniella pleaded to ride on horseback behind Julian. She made such a wheedling nuisance of herself that Lidi let her do it. The child perched on the saddle, arms happily clasped around Julian's waist. The Added Attraction, Lidi suspected, had found an added hero.

They crossed the border at sundown. Lidi insisted on going farther until they were well into Alto-Trento. They slept a few hours, set off again, and by midmorning halted at the outskirts of a market town.

"The *carabinieri*'s horses," Jericho went on. "I'm thinking we sell one, keep the other in case of need. We'll have money for food until we put on another show."

"I'll do a show as soon as I have a new act," Lidi said. "Something different, so the audience comes back for a second night. Maybe a third. Yes, sell one horse. The money will tide us over."

"I'll ride into town and see what I can do," Jericho said.

"I'll go with you," Julian offered. For the past day and more, he and the canvasmaster had kept their distance. Jericho finally talked to him apart. Though he would rather have been stretched on a rack than apologize, for Lidi's sake he wanted no bad feelings between them; so he managed to grumble that he hadn't meant to doubt the lad's word. Julian nodded. That settled it.

"I know how to dicker with them," Julian added. "You're an outlander. These horse traders will fleece you."

"Not me they won't," Jericho said. "I was dealing in horses before you cut your first tooth. I never got the short end of a bargain. Besides, they're stolen. It's all pure profit."

"He'll stay here, then," Lidi said. "He can learn 'The Condemned Prisoner.' That's the kind of act I need."

"No matter what," Julian said to him before the canvas-master rode off, "be sure you let them think they got the better of you. Even if they didn't. Especially if they didn't. It makes them happy. They'll brag about it for weeks. You'll be doing them a favor."

"Crazy country," Jericho said. "I'm beginning to like it."

Lidi motioned for Julian to come to the property wagon. Daniella, having watched her other hero ride out of sight, tagged after them.

"You won't mind having your head cut off?" Lidi said.

"Is that what you do to a first-of-May?"

"She won't really cut off your head," said Daniella. "It's just a trick."

"That's how you make your living?" Julian said to Lidi. "People pay you to fool them?"

"They understand that it's just make-believe. They love it. Jericho says it makes life easier to put up with. It's consoling."

"I wouldn't know," Julian said.

Lidi went behind the curtained alcove at the back of the wagon. She gathered up her equipment for "The Condemned Prisoner" and other small effects. Julian looked puzzled at the wooden framework, a metal blade, and a canvas bag.

"See if Jericho has any more paint," she told Daniella. "We'll put this together outside. It's a good effect," she said to Julian as the child trotted off to the tent wagon. "You'll see how it works."

"Are you going to show me all your secrets?" Julian said.

"Not all."

She had brought her deck of cards. Not an easy sleight, but she could do it well. She wanted to astonish him. It seemed important, even necessary. She cut and shuffled the cards with one hand. A quick turn of her wrist and they were blank pieces of pasteboard; another turn and she was holding a paper fan.

She had meant to astonish him. He astonished her. He threw back his head and laughed. His face brightened. She caught a glimpse of what he must have looked like when he was a boy.

"I didn't think you ever laughed," she said. "As a matter of principle."

"Jericho was right," he said. "It's consoling."

"You feel consoled?"

"Some. I'll need more." He grinned at her. "Do that again."

Lidi shook her head. "One rule: Never the same thing twice in a row."

"I can't believe what I saw."

"That's the point. You saw it. It's impossible. You can't believe it. You believe it anyway." Lidi made the fan disappear, which astonished him again.

"When I was little," she said, "I used to think I could do real magic. If I worked as hard as I could, put all my mind to it, and did a trick absolutely perfectly—it would really happen. I could turn paper flowers into real ones. I could even make myself vanish and be somewhere else far away."

"You still think so?" Julian said, halfway teasing.

Lidi smiled. "Maybe. It doesn't matter. Some illusions are so good they might as well be true."

She told him, then, about the rope trick. "My father said I'd never be a good magician if I didn't learn it. So I thought I had to learn it, just to show him I'd be better than he ever was. I don't care about that anymore, it makes no difference, it's got nothing to do with him. I want to learn it because it's the best trick in the world."

"A matter of principle?"

"More than that," Lidi said. "Sometimes I think my life's got itself tangled up with the rope trick."

"And mine," Julian said, "mine's tangled up with the Baboon."

"Yes," Lidi said, "and neither one of us can get loose. I have to find a magician named Ferramondo. He's the only one who knows how to do the trick.

"I'm looking for a town—Montalto," she added. "He might be there."

"You shouldn't have any trouble," Julian said. "We only have a few dozen Montaltos. It means 'high mountain.' So if a town has a bump in the road, it gets called Montalto, and everybody walks up and down admiring it. A crazy country, but we like it that way."

"My father told me it was in the south."

"Ah," Julian said. "That makes things easier. In the south, they only have maybe ten or twelve Montaltos. That cuts it down a little."

"I'll find it."

She had, meantime, taken out the silver coin she used for

"The Miser's Dream." As Julian watched, she made it jump back and forth across her knuckles, quicker than his eyes could follow, then held it between her thumb and forefinger.

"Watch carefully," she said.

The silver piece vanished.

Julian laughed again. "Will you teach me the trick?"

"Sometime."

Julian took her hands and kissed them, first one then the other.

"Why did you do that?" Lidi said.

"I asked you the same thing. I do what I do. That's what you told me then."

"I don't make a habit of it," Lidi said.

"Neither do I."

Daniella was back with some paint pots. Lidi and Julian picked up the framework and the rest of the gear and carried it outside.

"I could use a cabbage," Lidi said as she began fitting the pieces together.

"There may be one in the food sacks. I'll go and look," Julian said. "I'm just a first-of-May, but I think I can recognize a cabbage when I see one."

While he went to search, Lidi set the metal blade between the upright wooden slats and slid it up and down. She was satisfied the equipment worked smoothly.

Daniella's eyes followed Julian, who had gone to rummage among the provisions.

"He's in our family now," Daniella said.

"I don't know if he wants to be."

"He does." Daniella nodded. "And you'll love him forever."

"That," Lidi said, "is the silliest thing I've ever heard." Her hands suddenly shook and she nearly dropped the blade. "Get along with you, imp. No more such nonsense."

Daniella shrugged. "You will."

Lidi brushed away Daniella's remark and went back to examining the equipment, trying to keep her mind on her work, finding herself paying no attention to it. She was still tinkering, distracted, when Julian came back empty-handed.

"No cabbage," he said.

"Cabbage?" Lidi looked blankly at him. "Oh—that. Yes, well, never mind." Her cheeks, she knew, were flushed. She hoped he did not notice. "What happens, you see, if I had one—I'd put it on this block and slice it in half. That shows the audience the blade really cuts."

"So we need a cabbage?"

"Oh, forget the damned cabbage," Lidi burst out. "The main thing, Jericho brings you onstage. You're the condemned prisoner. You struggle, make believe you're terrified. Then Jericho slides the blade down and chops off your head."

"I sincerely hope you know what you're doing."

"Your head drops into the basket," Lidi went on. "With luck, somebody screams and faints. I make a big show of being in despair. Finally, I spread my cape over your dead body; you jump up good as new, everyone cheers, we take our bows—"

"What about my head?"

Lidi opened the bag and took out a wooden form with nose and ears. "This is you. Or will be when I paint it. I'll put a red bandanna on it. You'll wear one just like it. The audience won't notice the difference. They're too busy being shocked.

"It's easy, but we have to do it just right." Lidi showed him a shelf at the bottom of the frame. "The dummy's already there. When you kneel down, you slide it onto the block. And duck your own head in here." She pointed to an open space. "But you have to move fast. I twirl my cape to hide you when you make the switch. The basket has a false bottom. The audience thinks your head disappeared—"

Lidi stopped. Her silver coin—it suddenly occurred to her she had forgotten to put it back in her box of effects. She had palmed the coin and slipped it into a skirt pocket.

The pocket was empty.

12

Pompadoro's Performing Porkers

LIDI RUMMAGED IN HER OTHER POCKETS. She shook out the folds of her skirt to see if the coin had caught in the hem.

Julian watched her efforts. "Is this part of the act?"

"No," she said curtly. She was vexed at her carelessness. This had never happened before. "I can't find my silver coin. It's gone."

"You made it disappear," Julian said. "You never brought it back."

"It's just a trick." She stopped short of calling him an idiot. "It has to be here. Somewhere."

She scanned the ground, peered at the clumps of grass. "It must be in the wagon."

It was not. Exasperated, she went over every inch of the floor. She called Daniella, whose fingers were thin enough to poke into all the nooks and crannies. There was no sign of it. She went back to comb the ground again.

"What's it matter?" Julian said. "Don't you have another one?"

"It was my special silver piece. I always use it."

"It isn't lost," Daniella said.

"If I can't find something, I call that lost." Lidi rounded on Julian. "And you. You took my mind off what I was doing."

"I'm glad," Julian said. "I meant to. Besides, you had the coin last. I was just there being consoled."

"If you hadn't—"

"All right, then. I'm sorry I did."

"No, you're not."

"No, I'm not," Julian said.

"You're going to argue now?" Daniella said.

"What we're going to do," Lidi said, "is just shut up. Everybody."

Jericho was back soon after that. He found Lidi and Julian making a point of ignoring each other. Daniella ran to him as he swung down from the horse and unloaded the bags slung across the saddlebow.

"You were right," he said to Julian. "That horse trader took me for an outlander fool. He thought he'd skinned me alive, but it was the other way 'round. He was so tickled with himself, imagining he swindled me, he practically apologized.

"I came out of that bargain with money for a couple weeks' rations. And plenty left over." Jericho showed Lidi a handful of coins.

A silver piece glinted amid the coppers.

"How did you get this?" She picked it up from the heap. Her hand shook when she touched it.

"Money from selling the horse," Jericho said. "No, wait, let me think. I got some change back when I bought rations. The grain merchant, the baker—I don't know."

The canvasmaster scratched his head. "That's odd. I keep an eye on my money. I never noticed this until you saw it. What's wrong? You look seasick."

"Nothing wrong," Lidi said. "I just mislaid the coin I use for 'The Miser's Dream.'"

"No great matter," Jericho said. "Now you have another." He motioned to Julian. "Let's pack away those bags."

Lidi studied the piece, turning it over and over. She paced up and down in front of the wagon.

Daniella tagged after her. "I told you it wasn't lost."

"It's not the same one."

"Yes, it is," Daniella said.

Lidi clenched her hand so tightly the rim of the coin bit into her palm. "It can't be mine."

She knew it was.

———

They headed southward for the rest of that week. During the days, she tried to convince herself it hadn't happened. Her business was to know what was possible and what was not. A coin could not vanish, travel a few miles away, and come back again. But it did, and she had no explanation for it. Nights, troubled, she slept badly.

Everything put her out of sorts. Daniella fretted, impatient to play the Added Attraction. Jericho pressed her to set up another show. When she practiced "The Condemned Prisoner" with Julian, he sometimes dropped the dummy head before sliding it onto the block, or tripped when he was supposed to spring up alive. He only grinned and shrugged his shoulders, which exasperated her. She decided he was a hopeless, irritating bumbler. She wondered if she was in love with him.

Later, one of the draft horses pulled up lame. Another time, a wheel broke and took most of a day to fix. In a summer cloudburst, the roof of the property wagon sprang a leak. It was all a mess. She wondered if he was in love with her.

Then came the pigs.

After a night of tossing and turning, by morning she finally dozed off. Daniella shook her awake.

"Come see the piggies!"

"You're dreaming." Lidi pulled the covers over her head. "No piggies."

Daniella tugged at her until she rolled out of the cot. She heard squeals from the clearing. She was not up to dealing with pigs.

Julian and Jericho lounged against the tent wagon like a couple of street idlers, arms folded, doing nothing but looking on and laughing. Lidi counted eight or more half-grown pigs milling around the clearing, rooting into everything. Daniella, enraptured, scampered after them.

"Why are pigs here?" Lidi said.

She climbed down the wagon steps to shoo them away. One raced by and nearly bowled her over; the others wheeled about, jostling each other, squealing enough to give her a headache.

A man approached her from the roadside. A bright red fez with a dangling tassel perched on a head mostly made up of round cheeks and a mustache curling to his ears. A long, embroidered vest hung open to show a belly that strained to escape from the sash around his middle.

He beamed fondly at the frolicking pigs and made coaxing noises. They immediately dashed toward him, plumped down on their haunches in a circle, ears cocked attentively. Lidi had never seen smiling pigs.

"Signorina . . ." The new arrival raised his fez with a grand gesture. "I see you've met the porkers. Forgive their enthusiasm; they're high-spirited fellows. We enjoy a morning ramble. It benefits our digestion and keeps us in trim. From time to time, they root out a truffle or two, which they generously share with me.

"Pompadoro," he added, as if it were explanation in itself. "A name, perhaps, familiar to you?"

Lidi shook her head. "I can't say it is. Sorry."

"No need for apology," Pompadoro said. "You would be surprised how many are in that same unenlightened position. I am, however, in the way of correcting it."

He waved a hand at the smiling circle. "Pompadoro's

Performing Porkers. They will, I am confident, soon become a household name. The process, I can happily attest, is already taking place."

Pompadoro's glance fell on the property wagon and its painted lettering. "'Princess Lidi's Magical Mystifications'? Signorina, is it possible we follow the same profession?"

"I'm the Added Attraction," Daniella said.

"Of course you are," Pompadoro said. "You would add an attraction wherever you lend your graceful presence."

"I mean I'm *the* Added Attraction."

"I look forward to learning what it is that you attract," Pompadoro said. "But, my dear *principessa,* since we are colleagues, I would be honored to make the acquaintance of the rest of your troupe."

Jericho and Julian stepped forward as Lidi beckoned. "My canvasmaster," she said. "And my stage assistant—of sorts."

"Delighted." Pompadoro bowed elegantly. "And all the others in your equipage?"

"That's my equipage," Lidi said. "We travel light."

"So it would appear," said Pompadoro, casting an eye on the wagons. "Very light indeed."

"What about your own troupe?" Lidi said. "I've heard of trained bears and monkeys. But—performing pigs?"

"I'm a first-of-May in this business," Julian said, "but I know something about livestock. Where I come from, we have a saying: 'Never try teaching a pig to whistle. It's a waste of your time and it annoys the pig.'"

"In the case of the porkers, I admit they do not whistle,"

said Pompadoro. "But I have no doubt they would do so if they wanted, and put their minds to it. And what minds they have! The level of their intelligence approaches sublime heights. They enjoy dancing, acrobatics, playing musical instruments—"

"You taught them all that?" Lidi said.

"I would not call it a pedagogical exercise," Pompadoro said. "Rather, mutual agreement. I merely suggest, they do what they please. If you wish to see us perform, my company is set up hardly a quarter mile away. You are most welcome to observe—admission free, of course, as a professional courtesy.

"Permit me to ask," he added, "if you have breakfasted. No? Give us the pleasure, then, of joining us for a modest repast."

"I'd like that," Daniella said.

"Be assured," Pompadoro said, "no ham or sausage will be served. I myself abstain from meat of any sort—out of respect for the porkers' sensitivity, you understand."

While the canvasmaster and Julian followed in the wagons, Lidi set off on foot with Pompadoro. The porkers, Daniella among them, frisked on ahead.

"What a pleasure to encounter another artiste in such proximity," said Pompadoro as they strolled along. "An amazing coincidence—no, I should not employ that term. If coincidence implies an accidental conjunction of random events, there is no such thing.

"Consider the world as a grand loom," he went on. "Its threads, sooner or later, will inevitably cross. Therefore, what we call coincidence is simply the weaving of a pattern. If we could see the whole pattern, we could no doubt observe how these things come about. We are, unfortunately, too close to appreciate the larger aspects."

"Interesting. I never looked at it that way," Lidi said. "You've given it a lot of thought."

"I? Goodness, no," said Pompadoro. "I seldom think much about anything—except, of course, the porkers. I merely go about my business. This was told to me by a remarkable individual. As a professional, you will surely know his name: the Fantastic Ferramondo."

13

Pompadoro's Travels

"YES, NONE OTHER THAN FERRAMONDO himself," Pompadoro declared. "What a splendid fellow! He has my unceasing gratitude."

"Pompadoro," Lidi, jolted, hurriedly broke in, "tell me what you know about him."

"With utmost pleasure," said Pompadoro. "Thanks to Ferramondo, the porkers and I discovered each other. You shall observe the consequences of that momentous encounter."

Pompadoro guided her to a grassy meadow. His establishment, she saw, was more elaborate than her own. A crew of roustabouts heaved at the guy ropes of a large circular tent. Wagons of various sizes stood in the backyard. Performers in rehearsal clothes practiced cartwheels and back flips or gossiped around steaming canisters of food. Lidi was hungrier than she thought.

"You shall meet my artistes in due course." Pompadoro halted at a folding wooden table and canvas chairs in front of a red wagon Lidi assumed was his personal quarters—and, she supposed, the porkers' as well. "First, the promised repast."

Julian and Jericho parked the wagons in Pompadoro's backyard. Daniella raced up along with the porkers to join Lidi. Pompadoro, meantime, had gone into his vehicle. He popped out again with more breakfast dishes than Lidi had seen for weeks. The porkers waited, bright-eyed, as Pompadoro ladled portions into their bowls. Serving his guests, he constantly urged them to eat, and set himself as an example to follow.

"What you see around you," Pompadoro said between mouthfuls, "is merely the beginning of an enterprise grander than anything I could have imagined. I have, little by little, acquired my troupe of performers, and expect to add more in the course of time.

"The horizons are unlimited." Pompadoro fixed his gaze on some point in the distance. "I see them reaching beyond the borders of Campania. Who knows how far? This modest establishment will grow—"

"Your porkers are going to grow, too," Julian put in. "They get big, you know. Then what?"

"So much the better. All the more spectacular." Pompadoro loosened the sash around his middle. "I also entertain the fond hope they will produce generation after generation—"

"I'm sure they will," Lidi interrupted. "Can we talk about Ferramondo?"

"Always a pleasure to do so." Pompadoro settled himself in his canvas chair. "What is your particular interest?"

"I'm trying to find him."

"Ah. Indeed." Pompadoro shook his head. "*Principessa,* if you are trying to find him, there is, I fear, every likelihood that you will not. I have the impression that *you* do not find Ferramondo. *He* finds you."

"You talked as if you knew him," Lidi said.

"I doubt that anyone knows all there is to know about Ferramondo," Pompadoro said. "Would you care to disclose why you happen to be looking for him?"

"I want to learn how to do the rope trick," Lidi said.

"As do we all." Pompadoro chuckled. "Is there a magician in the world who wouldn't give his eyeteeth to know the secret, or even to see it performed? I myself hoped the same thing. I believed it would mend my fortunes, which, at the time, were in a generally emaciated condition."

Pompadoro rested his hands on his expansive midsection. "You may find it difficult, in view of my present circumstances, to believe I once lived a hand-to-mouth existence. The hand, alas, was most often empty, and very little made its way into the mouth."

"You must have put on weight since then," Jericho said.

"Quite so," said Pompadoro. "Before that, however, my career had been performing tricks at country fairs. A few sleights and vanishings, the usual repertoire. I did them badly. I was reduced, finally, to the infamous three-card monte."

"What's that?" Julian whispered to Lidi.

"You put two black aces and a red queen facedown on a table," Lidi said. "Move them around and bet no one can pick out the queen. It's a cheat, no better than robbery. You palm the queen, she isn't there to begin with. So you always win. Foolproof. Impossible to lose."

"I lost," Pompadoro said. "I continually fumbled the cards. The dullest yokel found the queen immediately. Despite my assiduous efforts to hoodwink the onlookers, I ended up penniless.

"I took to the road with all my worldly goods on my back, and, in my head, not the slightest notion of how I should make my living. For quite some time, I scraped along as best I could.

"One day, by coincidence—I use that word only as a convenient term—I met another traveler. A large, stout fellow with ruddy cheeks and a mustache that curled up to his ears. He had a wide-brimmed hat cocked on his head and an old cloak flapping at his heels. He carried a staff as tall as himself and walked beside a donkey cart—one of those peasant carts with big iron-shod wheels and painted all over with flowers and grapevines."

"I know the kind," Julian said. "We have them at home."

"We introduced ourselves," Pompadoro continued, "and you can be sure I was taken aback when I learned he was none other than the Fantastic Ferramondo. As we both were going in the same direction, he suggested we travel a little while together.

"I happily agreed, and, as it turned out, we got on like old friends. He even joked about his size. 'Pompadoro,' he'd say, patting his stomach, 'wherever I go, this gets there three minutes earlier.'

"He had a store of traveler's tales to split your sides laughing. For all that, he was a deep sort of fellow. I didn't understand half what he was talking about, but it passed the time.

"He had this notion about the world being like cloth on a big loom. Sooner or later, all threads cross. 'So you see,' he told me, 'there are no coincidences. There are only consequences. Everything has consequences. Touch one part of a spiderweb, the whole thing trembles. A butterfly flaps its wings at one end of Campania, there's a storm at the other.

"'But the cloth isn't woven as tight as you might suppose,' he said. 'If you know how, you can go through the threads, so to speak. Once you do that, everything is possible. You could likely walk through a brick wall, if you were interested in that sort of thing, and put your mind to it.'

"I said a person would have to put his mind to it pretty hard if he wanted to walk through a wall. 'Yes, up to a point,' he said. 'Beyond that, you don't think, you simply do.'

"He told me, in his travels, he'd seen magicians walk barefoot over hot coals. Or charm a cobra. Or break a plank of wood into splinters with the turn of a hand. They understood how to go through the threads. You just need to be in the right frame of mind.

"I asked him what frame of mind he was talking about. He thought it over awhile. 'Pompadoro,' he said, 'let me ask you a highly personal question: Were you ever in love?' I admitted, yes, I once lost my heart to a charming signorina. Alas, for one reason or another, nothing came of it.

"'That doesn't matter,' he said. 'Can you remember how you felt? Being in love? It's something like that.'

"This was all too deep for me," Pompadoro said. "But, since we'd been getting along so well, I finally ventured to ask him to do his famous rope trick.

"He only burst out laughing so hard I thought his mustache would fall off. 'Everybody wants to see the rope trick,' he said, after he got his breath back. 'I seldom perform it these days. It's too easy. So simple a child could do it. I'd even say a child could probably do it better than his elders. Some other time, perhaps.'

"I was disappointed. I hoped he'd change his mind," said Pompadoro. "But we parted company then. He had business elsewhere, and I had no business at all.

"He went his way, I went mine," Pompadoro said. "Soon after that, by coincidence—that is, by no coincidence—I passed a farm with a mucky, foul pigsty near the roadside. As soon as they saw me, those bedraggled pigs all began squealing, putting their little trotters through the rails as if they were beckoning to me. I stopped to have a look at them. Poor creatures, I knew they were doomed to be slaughtered.

"I swear to you," Pompadoro said, "in my mind I could hear them pleading, begging me for help. I was tempted to pull down the bars of the pen and set them loose. But I realized that would be a criminal offense, and so I didn't do it."

"A matter of principle," Julian said.

"No. A matter of fear," said Pompadoro. "I was afraid I'd be caught and hanged. So I told them, speaking with my thoughts, as it were, that I was heartbroken for them. I would have dearly loved to save them—but what could I do?

"I begged them to forgive me and I turned away. I'd hardly gone a dozen paces when I stopped. Against the law or not, I had to rescue them. I turned back.

"Can you imagine what they were doing? The dear creatures were climbing on one another's back, like a pyramid of circus acrobats. The smallest at the top jumped over the rails, then the others; the biggest and strongest at the bottom scrambled out as if they were going up a ladder.

"They raced to join me as fast as their trotters could carry them. They capered around, grunting with sheer joy. I expected they'd go their own way, but, no, they refused to leave my side. I still felt some uneasiness about being caught and hanged, so together we left the vicinity in haste. We have been inseparable ever since. The consequences, as Ferramondo would put it, were: Pompadoro's Performing Porkers, the beginning of our fortune, the foundation of our entire enterprise, all thanks to my lucky encounter with him."

"Did you ever see Ferramondo again?" Lidi asked.

"I regret to say I did not. Nor do I know of anyone else who has laid eyes on him. I realize we most value the advice of those who tell us what we want to hear," Pompadoro added, "but allow me to offer a small suggestion: Give it up."

14

Two Roads Meet

"NOT THAT I MEAN TO INTRUDE in someone else's business," Pompadoro said. "Meddling is an irresistible but thankless activity. Nevertheless, as one colleague to another, I feel obliged to express my concern. I fear you have embarked on a wild-goose chase."

"So I've been told." Lidi gave Jericho a dry smile. "But it's not all that wild. I know where to start. A town called Montalto. Julian here tells me there's a few dozen with the same name. If I have to, I'll go to every one."

"Montalto?" Pompadoro raised his eyebrows. "You should have mentioned that before. True, we have dozens of them. Logically, only one seems likely. I have never been there, but I know it by reputation. A certain quarter of the town is nicknamed 'Magicians' Burghetto.'

"For years, magicians, conjurers, street performers of all sorts have made their way to Montalto. To rest, polish their acts, sun themselves in peaceful retirement. On occasion—it grieves me to say this—some in our profession find it conveniently beyond reach of the long arm of the law. A good many reside there permanently. It's an out-of-the-way sort of place, ideal for all those purposes.

"The Burghetto keeps to itself. The rest of the town, however, finds it enjoyable to visit, for a family outing and entertainment. For you, *principessa,* it may well be a source of information."

"Where exactly is it?" Lidi said.

"Some way south," Pompadoro said. "A few miles beyond a market town—what's it called?—Malvento. Yes, near the Ardita Vecchia province.

"Is there some difficulty?" Pompadoro added, seeing Julian stiffen.

"No," Julian said. "Only that I was born and raised in Ardita Vecchia. I never heard of the Burghetto."

"Not surprising," said Pompadoro. "It's practically unknown to outsiders. They prefer it so."

"We'll find it," Lidi said. "Thank you, Pompadoro. You've made the wild-goose chase a bit less wild. And thank you for the pleasure of meeting the porkers."

"For breakfast, too," said Daniella.

"Let's be on our way," Lidi said to Jericho. "We can put in a good day's travel—"

"One moment." Pompadoro raised a hand. "It occurs to me, by coincidence—that word again—my company is also heading south. For a time, at least. Then we plan on turning toward the coast and passing a restful winter there. The porkers have never visited Campania's balmy seashore; it will be a treat for them. Until our paths diverge, I invite you to travel with us.

"Hear me out," Pompadoro said as Lidi was about to refuse. "In addition to the porkers, I have several acrobats and tumblers. A tightrope walker. A splendid contortionist—a gentleman who can fold himself small enough to fit into a picnic basket. An excellent diversity of talents.

"One essential is lacking: a magician. Especially a magician who is also a charming young woman; most unusual, I daresay altogether unique."

"She's good at it," said Julian.

"Of that, I have no doubt whatever," said Pompadoro. "Now, the porkers and I do our turn last, as the grand finale. I offer you the opening number. An enviable position on the program, presently occupied by our contortionist. But he's a flexible fellow, as it were; I'm confident he won't object."

"And the Added Attraction?" said Daniella.

"Of course." Pompadoro smiled indulgently. "What is it precisely that you attract?"

"I tell people things," Daniella said.

"Their fortunes?" Pompadoro turned to Lidi. "She's a palm reader? Clairvoyant? Mentalist? Always a surefire draw. I assume you've taught her all the tricks of the trade."

"No," Lidi said. "I taught her nothing."

"I just do it," Daniella said.

"A natural? Marvelous, quite rare. We shall gladly accommodate her. Regarding financial arrangements, we can surely reach a happy agreement."

"Thank you just the same. We'll be going—"

"A word in your ear," Pompadoro said when Julian and Jericho started for the wagons. "As this is none of my business, I am reluctant to insert my nose where it may be unwanted. Nevertheless, I feel a keen obligation toward a fellow artiste.

"I hear talk, around and about, of a dangerous criminal fugitive with a substantial reward attached to his head. A young felon, they say, on the run from Ardita Vecchia. Gossip, of course, is always highly exaggerated. But here— a simple coincidence?—I see a young first-of-May who, by chance, happens to come from that very province. Significant? Merely accidental?"

"It's not exactly what you think. I can explain."

"Speak not." Pompadoro put a finger to his lips. "Tell me nothing. I don't wish to know. I only point out—hypothetically, nothing personal—if an individual were to avoid scrutiny by the eye of the law, or the grasp of reward seekers, where better to do so than a circus? Costumes, greasepaint. Hiding in plain sight, if you will. We artistes, as you well know, are all one happy family—except, naturally, when we attempt to upstage each other. This individual, if there is such an individual, would be safe with us, lost for all practical purposes in the midst of our caravan.

"And so you could offer what I need to enhance my program. I could provide the anonymity this individual needs to avoid the unwelcome termination of his existence. I might further theorize that a young lady—a hypothetical young lady—would have a personal interest in the well-being of that individual. I trust I make myself clear."

"You're persuasive," Lidi said.

Jericho was checking the harness when Lidi went to him. "Unhitch the horses," she said. "After what Pompadoro told me, I changed my mind. We're staying with him. Awhile, anyhow.

"Your fame seems to have spread," she added to Julian. "People are still looking for you beyond Ardita Vecchia."

"I can take care of myself," Julian said.

"No doubt," Jericho said. "And the rest of us? You're a first-of-May, you do as you're told."

"One thing I didn't expect," Lidi said. "I never thought I'd be the opening act for a herd of dancing pigs."

———

The pigs danced that night. Pompadoro had advised Lidi to take a day or two of rehearsal and get used to her new working conditions. "We have close to a full house tonight. I urge you to attend the performance from the midst of the audience, where you can best observe the impact of the whole vast panorama."

The vast panorama was vast on a modest scale. Pompadoro, as ringmaster, had squeezed himself into a starched shirt and long-tailed coat. He strode back and forth, waving his arms as if he meant to embrace the entire audience, promising wonders never seen before.

"I doubt that," Lidi whispered to Julian, "but if he believes it himself, so will everybody else."

Still, she had to admit that the tall, gaunt gentleman in black tights—Flexo the Flexible—did fold himself into a picnic basket. The spectators cheered him, as they cheered the spangled acrobats and tumbler, the lady bareback rider, and the daring tightrope walker.

Jericho, who had seen such acts a thousand times, yawned. Daniella bounced up and down, clapping her hands. And Julian—Lidi remembered the day she had first seen him laugh; he had, now, the same boy's look of wonder. She remembered that was also the day he had kissed her hands.

Pompadoro vanished behind a canvas screen. He was back moments later, wearing his red fez, embroidered vest, and sash, as well as a cape glittering with sequins, from which he produced a battered fiddle and began scraping away.

Through an open flap at the rear of the tent, the pigs dashed to join him. They circled around first in one direction then the other. The audience cheered as they stood on their hind legs and twirled like ballet dancers. Pompadoro, light-footed despite his bulk, capered amid the porkers.

While Pompadoro squeaked out a livelier tune, the pigs leaped over one another's backs and did rolling somersaults. They lined up, finally, and bobbed their heads to acknowledge the wild applause. Pompadoro bowed to the spectators, then to the porkers. The rest of his company reappeared to make their grand exit procession.

Waiting for the tent to empty, Lidi glanced at Jericho. The canvasmaster had been silent, arms folded, throughout the performance. Knowing he made a point of saying nothing good about anything if he could possibly help it, Lidi was surprised when he came out with the highest praise one professional gives another.

"Not bad," he said.

15

The Condemned Prisoner

"I HAVE TO DISAPPEAR," Lidi said, the next day.

"Why?" Julian had been carrying wooden panels from the property wagon to Pompadoro's tent. He abruptly set them down. "Why would you do that? If anyone has to disappear, it should be me."

"I'm talking about 'The Vanishing Lady.' It's a trick. Did you think I meant I'd really disappear?"

"I never know what you mean," Julian said.

They had spent the morning rehearsing her program. Jericho had put together a platform at the far side of the tent. It could be set up and taken down in a matter of moments to clear the way for acts that followed. The benches for the audience did not circle the ring completely;

they stopped short of the opening where the artistes entered and exited. Lidi wanted no spectators behind her. Jericho would also hang a backdrop, and draperies at both ends of the platform. Lidi made sure there were blind spots to keep the audience from seeing what she did not want them to see.

"It's a big tent," Lidi said. "I'll have to do some big effects. Later, you can help me with 'Between Heaven and Earth.' That's a good one, where I float in midair. It takes practice, though. If Pompadoro wants us to go on tonight or tomorrow, 'The Vanishing Lady' will be just fine."

"Now you'll show me all your secrets?"

"The ones you need to know."

"Not all?" Julian watched her fit the panels together. "I need to know them all."

"It wouldn't matter. Even if I showed you how the tricks worked, you still couldn't do them right. It's not what you do, it's how you do it. The attitude you have when you're on stage. Style."

"I have no style?"

"You have one all your own," Lidi said. "It won't help you with magic. For that, you have to believe what you're doing. If you believe, so will everybody else. Jericho told me you have to love the audience."

"How can you love an audience? There's too many of them," Julian said. "What if I just loved one?"

"That depends on who it is," Lidi said. Then, after a moment, she said, "Can you love anyone when you hate so much?"

"I don't hate anybody," Julian said.

"You hate the Baboon. Enough to kill him."

"Him. Yes," Julian said. He had not been thinking much about the Baboon. He had been thinking about Lidi. "I could try killing him without hating him. Purely a matter of principle."

"No. You can't." Lidi practically threw the words at him. "What if you do? You'll never get away. They'll hunt you down, they'll find you sooner or later. They'll kill you for it."

"That's the part I don't like."

"Let it go, then. Just let it go."

"I can't. He shot Renzo. He shamed me."

"Don't you care what happens to you? Or anyone else?"

"Who else?"

Lidi turned away. She wondered how he could be such a fool. She wondered why she loved him in the first place. She finished putting the panels together and hung a narrow door on hinges at the front. Julian watched, curious, as if he had forgotten what they had been talking about.

"It's a box," he said. "That makes you vanish?"

"You close the door after I step inside. Count to ten, then open it. Try to look surprised when you see it's empty."

"I'll be surprised," Julian said. "I'm surprised already. I don't see how you do it."

"Neither does the audience. Look here—the back panel swings open. I'm out even before you shut the door. I need a few seconds to go behind the backdrop. Then I circle around and run onstage from the other side."

"That's all there is to it? Simple as that?"

"Simple as that. Are you disappointed?" From the look

on his face, it suddenly dawned on her. "Oh, no—you really believed I could disappear into thin air?" Lidi began to laugh. "I think you did. Admit it. What a first-of-May you are!"

"Maybe I did, maybe I didn't," Julian said. "I never know what you're likely to do."

"Neither do I," said Lidi.

————

Later in the day, they finished rehearsing "The Condemned Prisoner." Julian had done his part perfectly, without fumbling the wooden head or getting himself stuck under the blade. Lidi was satisfied. It would, she decided, be the closing effect. Pompadoro came to find them in the tent. Lidi expected his porkers to be with him.

"They're resting," he explained. "A strenuous effort for them, as you've seen. They require a brief snooze before we go on."

"You told us they played music," Julian said. "Will they do it tonight?"

"Ah—yes. Well, no. Not exactly," said Pompadoro. "That is, they would—had I any instruments. When I acquire some, I can assure you they will perform on them most admirably.

"Along those lines," he added, "there is a small difficulty. Flexo the Flexible, I regret to say, is suffering from a sprained back. His joints, you see, are so loose they occasionally pop out; an occupational hazard for an artiste of his profession. I realize you've barely had time to work out your program, but I would be greatly obliged if you began tonight."

"We'll be ready," Lidi said. She hoped they would.

"Excellent," said Pompadoro. "Tomorrow, then, we shall pack up and move on. We've had a profitable run, but I find it doesn't pay to linger in one place overlong."

"I found that out, too," Lidi said.

Jericho, meanwhile, set up Daniella's pavilion beside the larger tent. Pompadoro had spread word of a child prodigy who saw through the veil of the future and offered prophecies at reasonable rates. He reckoned that townsfolk who had already seen the show would come for the Added Attraction; others might wish to consult her before the main performance. If demand was great, the Divine Daniella's services would be available during the show itself.

"I can't let her do that," Lidi said. "Someone has to be with her when I'm onstage. Jericho would keep an eye on her, but I need him to help me with 'The Condemned Prisoner.' He can't be in two places at once. Even I can't do that."

"He shall, indeed, watch over the charming Daniella," Pompadoro said. "I offer you the services of one of my roustabouts. A gentle soul, he tends to be rather muscular and hairy. A great personal sadness for him, since he appears to the superficial observer to be altogether villainous."

"I can work with that," Lidi said.

It was Julian who worried her. His moves were perfect in rehearsal. In front of an audience, he might come down with a paralyzing case of stage fright.

"If anything goes wrong," she told him, "don't let on. Improvise, make up something. They'll never know the difference."

To her relief, when Pompadoro introduced her act that night, Julian was calm, confident, and very handsome in his red bandanna. The audience cheered from the start and never stopped. She began, as she always did, with "Hands of Glory." She materialized bouquets of flowers, made solid steel hoops link together in a long chain. For "The Vanishing Lady," Julian allowed her exactly the time she needed to disappear and come back again to still louder applause.

She closed with "The Condemned Prisoner." Pompadoro's roustabout looked more villainous than usual; the audience hissed and booed when he led his prisoner to the fatal apparatus. While Julian made a show of struggling against his captor, Lidi flung herself about the stage, wringing her hands, pleading for mercy. Unmoved, the executioner forced Julian to the block and brought down the blade.

The wooden head thudded into the false bottom of the basket. The audience screamed. From the commotion at one side of the tent, Lidi guessed, with satisfaction, that someone had fainted or possibly thrown up. She turned over the basket, found it empty; then ran to Julian's side and swirled her cape across the motionless body.

The spectators cheered when Julian sprang up with his head miraculously on his shoulders. Before Lidi realized what he was doing, he flung his arms around her and kissed her. The audience roared approval mixed with heartwarming *aaw*s.

"This isn't part of the act." Lidi could hardly catch her breath. "Let me loose, you fool. What are you doing?"

"Improvising."

One of the roustabouts, that moment, set off the fireworks Jericho had rigged for Lidi's grand finale. The canvasmaster had packed a row of canisters with the chemicals Lidi used for "Hands of Glory," added black powder and phosphorus to send fountains of sparks streaming into the air. More cheers rattled Pompadoro's tent. Lidi and Julian stepped forward to take their bows.

"No encores," Lidi said from the corner of her mouth.

She hustled him off the platform. Much as she wanted to see Pompadoro and his dancing porkers do their act again, she was anxious for Daniella. Instead of waiting for the rest of the show and the grand exit procession, she headed for the child's pavilion.

"I'm going to like the magic business," Julian said, hurrying to keep up with her.

"Don't get to like it too much. You made a big mistake at the end."

"What mistake? There wasn't any mistake."

"You forgot to smile," she said.

16

Two Roads Part

"A MARVELOUS MOMENT!" Pompadoro was still flushed and sweating after his own performance. As soon as the show ended, he had come to the pavilion. His porkers frisked after him. The Added Attraction had been receiving one customer after another without pause. Jericho, seeing the child was overtired, had just called a halt to the consultations.

"That heartfelt embrace—the audience adored it," Pompadoro went on as Daniella hopped down from her stool to pat the porkers and tickle their ears. "Your program was delightful, as I knew it would be. And your 'Condemned Prisoner'—brilliant! An inspired touch at the end. A loving kiss—the greatest magic!"

"That was my idea," Julian said.

"I'm not surprised," Jericho muttered, when he understood what Julian had done.

"It was only stage business," Lidi said.

"Of course," Jericho said. "Only stage business."

"I urge you to incorporate it into future performances," Pompadoro said. "The audience will insist on it, and we artistes always bow to popular demand."

"A matter of principle?" Julian said.

"Good for the box office," said Pompadoro.

He bustled away to count the evening's receipts. The Added Attraction could barely keep her eyes open. While Lidi and Jericho collected the stage equipment, Julian carried the child to the property wagon. More asleep than awake, she murmured about wanting to play with the piggies. She suddenly turned her face to Julian.

"You're going," she said.

"We're all going with Pompadoro. You'll need to be up early and help us pack."

"I don't mean that." The Added Attraction looked deeply at him. "I mean you're going away from us."

"Of course I'm not," Julian said. "Why would you say that?"

"Because I know."

She was asleep by the time Julian brought her to the wagon.

———

For the next few weeks, Pompadoro followed easy roads that skirted the mountains. Eager to reach the seacoast, he stopped at fewer towns than Lidi expected. Even this far south, the breeze had an edge of autumn. Lidi watched the endless fields and vineyards, the clusters of tenants' cottages.

"The farther I run, the closer I get to where I started," Julian said. "This is like Malvento, where I come from. The *latifundia,* the great landholdings."

"Are they all so big?"

"Now, yes. Not always. The *latifundia* used to be common land. It belonged to all of us. No sharecropping, we kept what we grew. That was long ago, before we lost everything."

"How could you lose what you owned? What happened?"

"The *condottieri.* Soldiers for hire," Julian said. "Not much better than a gang of thugs. A little plundering here, a little throat cutting there. For a price. In the old days, there was fighting between the provinces. The farmers paid the *condottieri* to protect them. We hired the fox to guard the henhouse.

"They ended up gobbling everything for themselves. Then they did what every cutthroat dreams of." Julian gave a bitter laugh. "They became respectable. That was the start of our noble families. They all probably have a paid assassin for a great-grandfather."

"And nothing you can do?"

"Do what?" Julian said. "To make it all the worse, the land still belongs to us. It's ours. We own it. As we always did."

"I don't understand. If it's yours, why can't you get it back?"

"Because it's a crazy country. Yes, it's our land. That's what the law says. But the law also says we only get it back if the landholder dies."

"So? Your Marchese di Malvento can't live forever."

"He could try," Julian said. "And probably do it, too, out of spite. I wouldn't put it past him. But there's something else: The land goes to the tenants only if he dies without children to inherit it from him. Or, if he pleases, he can sell it.

"But there's usually a son or daughter he can pass it down to. The landholders make a point of having big families. A matter of principle.

"So do we," Julian added. "The difference is: Ours, we can't afford."

———

There were moments, as the caravan made its way over higher ground, when Lidi could see a glint of blue at the horizon.

"We're close to the sea," Pompadoro said. "The porkers can smell it. They're very excited. What a joy it will be to see them splashing in the surf."

"I'm sure," Lidi said.

For herself, she was sure of nothing. Sometimes, with Julian, she even forgot about Ferramondo and his rope trick, and simply let herself be happy. And that was the trouble.

Daniella, when she was not being the Added Attraction, spent her time with the porkers. They traipsed after her, as fond of her as they were of Pompadoro. She had become a favorite with the tumblers, the lady rider, and Flexo the Flexible. The child said nothing about it, but Lidi suspected she would have been content to stay with the troupe. Jericho and the roustabouts had grown to be close cronies. Unusual for him, the canvasmaster rarely grumbled; when he did, it was more a matter of keeping in practice. It was Julian who weighed on her mind.

It was full autumn now. Pompadoro was ready to turn toward the seacoast, to Basilia, where they would pass the winter. Lidi should have parted company with him long before. She kept putting it off. Julian never spoke about it. Neither did she. Finally, she made herself say it:

"I think you should stay with Pompadoro," she told him. "You'll be safer with him."

They were, that morning, in Pompadoro's tent. They had given their last performance the night before. The roustabouts had furled the canvas side panels and unbolted the wooden benches. A wind from the sea blew across the empty ground that still showed footprints of the grand exit procession.

"And then?" Julian said. "A first-of-May comes in the spring and goes in the fall. That's what you're telling me?"

"I'm going to Montalto. I have to. You know that. It's too close to your province. You can't risk it."

"I risk what I risk," Julian said.

"If you're with Pompadoro, I'll know where to find you. As soon as I'm back—"

"When?"

That was the question she did not want him to ask.

"Once I learn the rope trick."

"If you don't?"

That was the question she did not want to answer.

"I'll put together a whole new show," she went on quickly. "We'll do 'The Condemned Prisoner' and all the others. We'll have a mind-reading act, too. I'll show you how."

"I'd like to read your mind," Julian said.

"There isn't any mind reading, there's no such thing. It's just a trick. You go into the audience. Pick out somebody, ask them to hold something in their hand. I'm onstage blindfolded. I pretend to think about it for a few seconds, then I tell them what it is."

"How do you know?"

"You'll tell me," Lidi said. "It depends on the words you use. If you say, 'Here's a fine-looking gentleman,' that means he's holding a watch. If you say, 'This lady wants you to tell her . . .' that means she has a ring. Then if you say, 'Think hard. Concentrate,' that means it's a diamond ring. And so on. They're code phrases. You'll need to memorize a lot of them."

"I'll try it."

"I wrote some down, for a start." Lidi handed him a sheet of paper. "Read them out; you'll see how it works."

She went to sit on the edge of the platform, shut her eyes, and put a hand to her forehead. Julian scanned the page. As he called out the words that signaled each object, she answered him: a gold ring, a necklace, a locket. He was silent a moment. She waited. Then, his voice:

"I never want to leave you."

"I don't want you to," Lidi said.

She opened her eyes. Julian was looking at her.

"I gave you the signal for a diamond earring."

"No. You told me—" She stopped. "I heard you," she murmured. "I heard you—"

She slid down from the platform. "I don't want to do this anymore."

She turned to go. Julian took her by the shoulders. "What did you hear? What did you think I said?"

"You told me: 'I never want to leave you.'"

"You gave the right answer."

———

She found Pompadoro sitting at a folding table in his red wagon. The porkers lounged around him. He had taken off his fez and set it on a stack of papers. A pair of half spectacles perched on the end of his nose. He glanced over the rims at Lidi.

"Adding up the receipts," Pompadoro said. "Most excellent. Better than we've ever done."

"I'm glad." Lidi paused for a few moments. Then she said, "We'll be going to the Burghetto now."

"Ah. Yes." Pompadoro sighed. "As I supposed you would. And your first-of-May?"

"Julian, too."

Pompadoro's face fell. "Are you sure that's wise?"

"It's not wise. It's what he wants."

"I can't say I'm surprised." Pompadoro took off his spectacles and rubbed his eyes. He looked, for an instant, tired and troubled before he got back his usual high spirits. "I do admit the thought flickered through my mind—a glimmering hope—you might all stay with us. You've been shining additions to the troupe. Together, we could look forward to a dazzling future. Command performances in front of the crowned heads of the world; enthusiastic—and highly profitable—audiences in every nation's capital. I state with total confidence: That is a distinct possibility. I would even go so far as to call it a definite maybe.

"Whereas, and on the other hand," Pompadoro continued, "your wild-goose chase—forgive me for using the term—has every likelihood and probability of coming to naught. *Principessa*, I strongly urge you to reconsider."

Lidi shook her head. "I'm going there, no matter. I think Ferramondo knows a lot more than the rope trick. I want to learn whatever else he can tell me. But I'll say this: If it turns out I can't find Ferramondo, I'll come back to you. If I find him and he does teach me the trick, I'll still come back and show you how it works."

"I would, in times past, have been eager for that information," said Pompadoro. "Now I must tell you I'm not overwhelmingly interested. The porkers and I are perfectly happy. No doubt they could do it, but I see no great purpose in troubling them to climb up a rope and disappear." He patted his extensive paunch. "Nor would I care to do it myself. I thank you, nevertheless, for your offer."

Pompadoro opened a tin cash box. He filled a sack with

coins and handed it to Lidi. "For you, my dear. Your share of the takings."

"All that? So much?" Lidi hefted the sack. "More than generous."

"Only what's fair. You've earned every bit of it. Since your mind's made up, I wish you the best of luck. Travel well," he fondly added. "Be sure, whatever your circumstances, we shall welcome you with outstretched arms. In the case of Flexo the Flexible, literally so."

————

While Jericho stowed the last of the gear, Daniella lingered to say good-bye to the porkers. Lidi had already climbed onto the property wagon. Julian took the child in his arms to hoist her up.

"And you, Added Attraction," he said, teasing, "what did you tell me? I wouldn't stay with you? Admit it, you little imp. This time you were wrong."

"I'm never wrong," Daniella said.

17

The Magicians' Burghetto

MONTALTO, ONE OF THE OLD independent hill towns, paid no attention to the law of gravity. The cluster of white walls and orange rooftops clung to the high slopes out of sheer stubbornness. Lidi saw it rising in the distance a week after leaving Pompadoro's caravan. It took another two days before she came close enough to turn the wagons onto the road winding upward. Pompadoro's directions had been good, but he had not warned her how steep and narrow the track would be. To guide around the sharp turns and blind curves, Julian rode ahead on the *carabiniere*'s horse—stolen so long ago, it seemed, that Lidi had nearly forgotten it was stolen in the first place.

"From here," Julian said as they stopped to rest in the

chalky dust of the roadside, "you can almost see where I was born." He pointed farther south, beyond the mist drifting over the deep valleys. "I'm practically home again."

Lidi could not read his expression. From his voice, she could not tell whether he was wistful or bitter. His thoughts—there had been only that one moment in the tent when she heard them as clearly as if he had spoken. It frightened her. It had not happened again. She was glad of that. She said no more about it. Neither did Julian. She wondered if it frightened him, too.

They drove through what had once been a gate and the ruins of an ancient stone wall, and jogged into a sun-swept market square. Striped awnings hung over stands of fruit and vegetables hauled up from the terraces below. Shoppers and passersby, used to seeing caravans come and go, hardly glanced at the wagons.

Lidi reined up beside a fountain in the middle of the square. A woman with a bright-colored headcloth and full skirts was filling a couple of water buckets. She smiled and nodded when Lidi asked directions to the Magicians' Burghetto, but answered in a dialect that even Julian hardly understood.

"Here, they call it the Little Town. Sometimes the Old Town," Julian explained.

"Any chance she could help us?" Lidi said. "Has she ever heard of Ferramondo?"

The woman only shook her head and kept pointing downhill to a jumble of houses. Lidi set off again, and they squeezed the wagons past yet another ruined gate. A rabbit warren of plaster-walled buildings leaned against one another to keep from falling down, and all tilted toward the hillside to keep from falling off. On the rooftops, chimneys bent in more odd angles than Flexo the Flexible. Fire-eaters, sword swallowers, tumblers crowded the little piazza. Drummers tossed their drumsticks in the air and caught them again without missing a beat. Street musicians blared away on trumpets and trombones, Gypsy dancers rattled castanets, magicians produced bouquets of flowers out of thin air. Come for an afternoon's amusement, onlookers bought sausages and roasted chestnuts from strolling vendors. Like a conjurer's trick, more people crammed the piazza than it had room for.

The racket made Lidi's ears ring. She had no idea where to begin. As she tried to collect her wits, her only thought was to go from house to house, knocking on every door. The Burghetto had so many byways and side streets, she calculated it would take days to explore them all.

She halted the property wagon at the edge of the piazza and beckoned to Jericho. Daniella bounced up and down, eyes alight. Before Lidi could catch her, the Added Attraction jumped down and scurried into the press of onlookers and performers.

As much exasperated as alarmed, Lidi called to her. The noise from the piazza drowned out her voice. She hurried after the child. Daniella wiggled like a fish through the crowd.

Losing sight of her, Lidi jostled past the spectators. She shouldered her way from one end of the piazza to the other, circling around to find herself back at the wagons. She told Julian and Jericho to stay where they were and keep watch, and was about to start over.

Daniella came threading her way along the fringe of passers-by. Lidi collared her.

"Don't you ever—" Lidi gave up trying to scold the child. The Added Attraction was too caught up in the serious business of being delighted with herself to pay much attention.

"I was asking people about Ferramondo," she said.

Behind her, a boy in spangled tights had been walking on his hands. With his feet where his head should be, he waggled his legs in the air.

"He knows something," Daniella said.

The boy flipped himself right side up. He grinned and bobbed his head.

"True?" Lidi said to him. "Tell me."

"Soldi? Gelt? Dinero?" He rubbed a thumb against his fingertips.

"The universal language," Jericho said.

"I speak it perfectly." Lidi dipped into her purse and tossed the boy a coin. He caught it in midair and made it vanish into his ear.

"Merci beaucoup, nice lady." He took hold of the horse's bridle. *"Bellissima signorina,* you come *conmigo. Adelante! Avanti!"*

He swaggered into a narrow lane. Clotheslines stretched between the upper windows; red-and-green tights, baggy pantaloons hung like flags. The artistes had been doing their laundry.

The boy stopped at an open-fronted shed. He jerked a thumb toward a figure moving about in the shadows.

"Ferramondo?" Lidi whispered.

"*Nein, nein.* Mercurio. You *parlez* with him."

The boy cartwheeled off. Lidi stepped inside. The place had once been a stable. Now barrels, bottles, pots, pans, and double boilers jammed the stalls. A wooden worktable held flasks and beakers bubbling over flames from alcohol lamps. Mercurio was mopping up a puddle of bile-green liquid.

"You want rooms?" Mercurio put aside the mop. He wiped his hands on an apron that might have been, years before, white. He was hollow-cheeked, thin as a stick, with barely enough skin to cover his bones. "How many?"

"We don't need rooms—" Lidi began.

"What?" Mercurio's head went back as if Lidi had insulted him. "What's the matter with you, you don't want rooms? Everybody wants rooms. You're telling me you don't like my house?"

"It isn't that," Lidi said. "I'm looking for somebody. A magician—"

"Magicians all over the place. Don't bother me with magicians."

"His name's Ferramondo—"

"That fraud! That cheater!" Mercurio's cheeks flapped in and out. "I don't want to hear about him."

"But I do," Lidi said.

"That lurching bag of bones! That skulking skeleton!" Mercurio yelled. "And the same goes for his scruffy donkey. Jackasses, both of them! His monster cat, too."

While Mercurio ranted and flung himself around, Lidi glanced at Jericho. "Bag of bones? Ferramondo? Odd. Pompadoro said he was fat."

"Pompadoro?" Mercurio rounded on Lidi. "Pompadoro? I've heard of him. The pig fellow. What does he know? You want me to tell you what he knows? I'll tell you what he knows. What he knows is: Nothing!"

"Then," Lidi said, "that means you know something?"

"More than a fool who dances with pigs. More than I have a mind to jabber with you." Mercurio folded his arms and snapped his jaws shut.

"Try speaking the universal language again," Julian said under his breath to Lidi.

"Of course." She sighed and fished out a coin, and held it in front of Mercurio.

"Not worth my time." Mercurio snorted, pocketing the money.

"We'll see if it's worth mine," Lidi said.

18

Mercurio

DANIELLA, MEANTIME, HAD WANDERED over to Mercurio's table and watched the bubbles dancing in the flask.

"Get away from there!" Mercurio shouted. "You'll spoil my experiment."

"From the smell," Jericho said, "I think it's spoiled already."

"My fortune, that's what it is," Mercurio retorted. "Or will be. I'm onto the secret now."

"Good for you," Lidi said. "But it's not my interest—"

"I'm not some ordinary ignoramus, you know," Mercurio went on. "I've studied metamorphology, transmutation of base metals—"

"Alchemy?" Lidi said. "You can't believe you'll make gold from what you're cooking in those bottles."

"Of course not," Mercurio snapped. "Do you take me for a fool? Gold? Ridiculous. No, not gold. Diamonds.

"That's right. Diamonds," Mercurio said. "Why else would I keep a rooming house and waste my time taking in lodgers? You want to know? You're asking? All right, I'll tell you. I need the money for my experiments."

"You said you found the secret."

"Ah—not quite. Any day now. Oh, yes, the secret," he slyly added. "You'd like to know it, wouldn't you?"

"What I'd like to know about is: Ferramondo."

"It's the container. You need the right kind," Mercurio pressed on. "I can tell you that much, because it's no use to you. You'll never figure it out. Oh, I've tried crucibles, airtight barrels, even sauce pots and frying pans. I'm inventing my own distillation tubes—"

"Get to Ferramondo," Lidi said.

"What's to tell? Nothing worth wasting my breath on." Mercurio shrugged. "He came looking for a place to stay, and a stall for his knock-kneed donkey. I rented him the best room in the house. All right, all right, almost the best. I knew he was up to no good when he pays in advance. 'There's a suspicious character,' I say to myself. 'I'll keep an eye on that one.'

"He's hardly here a day when he takes in a stray cat. A long-legged, vicious black-and-white monster. Whenever that flea-bitten creature sees me, he gives me a big-eyed, impudent look. I swatted him with a broom once. And what does he do? He turns around and hisses at me, the vile-tempered creature.

"The two of them stayed in that room for days on end. Well, that's none of my business. But I worried about him, you understand. I was afraid he might be sick, so I kept banging on the door to ask what he's doing. He claimed he was trying to improve some trick or other."

"The rope trick?" Lidi pricked up her ears. "Did you ever see him do it?"

"A dozen times and more," said Mercurio. "When the mood struck him, he'd go into the piazza and put on a show. Even the other magicians stopped to look."

"There's a compliment," Jericho said.

"Exactly what did he do?" Lidi said. "How long was the rope? Coiled up? Stretched out? Did he just toss it into the air? How close was the audience?"

"If you're going to be picky about details," Mercurio said, "in the strict sense, technically speaking, I never actually saw it. I had better things to do. But I heard a lot about it."

"That's no help." Lidi shook her head. "Nothing else you can tell me?"

"I can tell you he cheated me, that's what," Mercurio retorted. "I was kind enough to be friendly and sociable and talk to him about my experiments. So clever, he's supposed to be? I thought he'd know something useful. But no! All he says to me is:

"'You mean to make diamonds? Out of—no offense intended—garbage? Why would you want to do that?'

"Foolish question if ever I heard one," Mercurio went on. "But I answer him, 'Because they're valuable.'

"'Why so?' he says to me.

"'People pay good money, that's why.'

"'Valuable to them,' he says, 'but the question is: Are they valuable to you?'

"And that's all I get out of him. But he's a sly one. He knows more than he lets on. I'm sure of it. He has this book, you see."

"What book?" said Lidi.

"His book with all his secrets. I've heard the gossip. They say everything he knows is in there. So, I think, 'All right, as you've been so disagreeable and unhelpful, I'll just have a look for myself.'

"Next time he's in the piazza, I go up to his room. The door's unlocked, I take a peek inside, and there it is lying on a pile of his junk. A big, ratty old book, so moldy you could grow mushrooms. And his cat sleeping on top of it.

"As soon as I go near, the beast wakes up, lays back his ears, and hisses. I'm ready to give him a smack and shoo him off. But that vicious monster spits and yowls, flies through the air, and gets his claws into me.

"I grab him by the scruff of the neck and try to peel him off. That very minute, curse the luck, who comes in? I'll tell you who comes in: Ferramondo.

"He clicks his tongue at the cat, the creature lets go of me and jumps on his shoulder. Ferramondo stands there looking very stern. I admit he's making me feel a little nervous. Who knows what he's likely to do?

"I tell him: No harm, no harm, I only wanted to borrow his book for a while.

"'Borrow without asking?' he says. 'Some people might call that stealing.'

"I knew I was in for it. I keep my mouth shut, hoping he won't set his cat on me—or worse. Then he gives me a silly idiot grin.

"'Now, see here, Mercurio,' he says. 'You don't want to be a thief. I don't want you to be one, either. You can have the book. Take it. Keep it. It's yours.'

"I don't need to be told twice. I pick it up and get out as fast as I can. I go into my storeroom, lock the door, and start reading.

"Then I see how he cheated me. The pages—blank! I spend hours turning every one. Empty! Not a word! Until I come to the last. And what's there? In little tiny letters at the bottom of the page:

The container is one thing; the contents, another. When you understand the difference between the vessel and what it holds, you take a step toward wisdom.

"Swindler!" Mercurio cried. "He gave me nothing! 'But,' I say to myself, 'I'll give him something. A good big piece of my mind.'

"I go to his room to tell him what I think of him. Nobody there. He's packed up and gone; him, his cat, and his donkey."

"And the book?" said Lidi.

"Threw it in the fire. What else would I do with trash?"

"Then?"

"That's it. That's all. I saw no more of him, good riddance. Enough for you?"

"Enough?" Lidi said. "Hardly. I want to know where to find him."

"Oh, I'll answer you that," Mercurio said. "You can't. Nobody can. For a good and simple reason."

"Which is?"

"Because," said Mercurio, "he's dead."

19

Cocofino

"THAT'S RIGHT," MERCURIO SAID. "As I've heard travelers tell it, he disappeared one day. Vanished into thin air. Gone from the face of the earth, never seen again. If that's not dead, it's near enough. You're sure you don't want to rent a room?"

Lidi turned away. Julian put an arm around her shoulder. "I'm sorry. It happens to people."

"The one thing I didn't expect," Lidi said. "I was sure I'd find him."

"Princess, you did your best," Jericho said. "If it's true as he says, no use looking anymore. Let it go at that."

"I'll have to let it go," Lidi said. "But I can't."

Daniella skipped ahead as they walked outside. A plump,

pink-cheeked little man in a flour-dusted apron perched on
the wagon step.

"Signorina . . ." He glanced inside the shed to make certain Mercurio had gone back to his worktable. He winked
and beckoned to Lidi.

"You're the one asking about Ferramondo?"

"How do you know that?" Lidi said.

"Word travels fast in the Burghetto, signorina."

"So it seems," Jericho said. "What, does everybody know
everybody else's business?"

"Indeed." The little man bobbed a head of bushy white
hair. He laid a chubby finger on the side of his nose. "But
some know more than others."

"That doesn't matter now," Lidi said. "I found out what
I didn't want to hear: Ferramondo's dead."

"Oh, I doubt that very much. You've been talking to
Mercurio? Pay no attention to anything he told you. Half
what he says is wrong, the other half's mixed up, and the
rest is nonsense. Talk to Mercurio? A waste of time. No, no,
you talk to me: Cocofino."

"I'm talking to you." Lidi sighed and dipped into her
purse.

"Money? No question of money." Cocofino waved a
hand. "My pleasure."

"My shock," said Jericho.

"Come to my pastry shop." Cocofino motioned for them
to lead the wagons to the piazza. "I don't like being too
long away from my pastries. A busy day."

"Will there be cake?" Daniella said.

"All you can eat, *piccina*. Or, if you like, jam tarts, apple puffs . . ." Cocofino grew animated, smacking his lips and kissing his finger ends. "Apple puffs, yes—so delicious. But they can be difficult. Shy, as you might say. You have to coax them to be flaky. Jam tarts, on the other hand—bold and brash, altogether immodest. I tell them: please, please, a little more restraint."

"One thinks he'll make diamonds out of swill," Jericho muttered. "Another talks to baked goods."

Cocofino chattered on about his wares. Reaching his shop, he ushered his visitors inside. As he had said, it was a very busy day. Customers pressed around the counter. A woman as plump as Cocofino cheerfully did her best to serve them all at once. Half a dozen youngsters filled trays with pastries that were bought as soon as they set them out. Cocofino spared only a moment to present his wife and family before darting to the kitchen and peeking into the oven.

Daniella blissfully inhaled the aromas of almonds and cinnamon. "Where's the cake?"

"Come, come." Cocofino beckoned them to join him. "Sit down quietly. It's the apple puffs, you see. Please, if you don't mind, no loud noises. They'll get upset and go soggy.

"As to Ferramondo," he went on, "it's been some while since we were together. Who knows what could have happened in the meantime? I can only assure you, when last I saw him, he was distinctly alive, no mistake about it. And Pistachio, as always, in the best of spirits."

"Pistachio?" Lidi said.

"His cat. The two of them were inseparable. Ah, that Pistachio. A big black-and-white fellow—"

"So Mercurio told me."

"A delightful creature," Cocofino went on. "Always ready with a purr. Liked to be tickled, he did. Rolled on his back, all paws waving. Yes, gentle as a lamb. But clever as a fox. And quick—well, quick as a cat, which he'd naturally be, wouldn't he?"

"That's a vicious monster?" Lidi whispered to Julian.

One of the youngsters came in with a tray of cookies and a splendidly decorated cake. Cocofino bustled about, serving portions, hurrying to his oven and back again.

"Forgive me. The jam tarts were getting rambunctious. Yes, now, where was I? Pistachio—"

"Ferramondo," Lidi put in. "You said you were together."

"Indeed so. At the time, I was a lad barely grown, doing odd jobs here in the Burghetto. Ferramondo had rooms in that foul-smelling house Mercurio kept. How the poor man put up with it, I'll never know. But he was such a mild-mannered little chap, never a word of complaint—"

"Little? I thought he was big," Lidi broke in.

"Not at all," said Cocofino. "Is that what Mercurio told you? Nonsense. A short, stubby-legged fellow, he was. A little moon face, hair like a dandelion gone to seed. For all his chubby fingers, he was so deft and quick. I've never seen anyone do tricks the way he did. Make your head spin, they would. Whenever I had a spare moment, I used to watch him in the piazza."

"Then you saw his rope trick?"

"No, I missed that one. I was busy running here and there, on all manner of errands, to make my living; and getting more kicks than tips. But he was remarkable. I'd look at him and say to myself: 'Cocofino, my lad, magic's your road to fame and fortune, and better than hard knocks.'

"It was in my mind every day, how I'd ask him to take me along and give me a few pointers, and set me on my way to being a magician, too. One morning, then, I saw him come into the piazza with his cart and donkey."

"At least you and Mercurio agree on the donkey," Lidi said.

"He was leaving the Burghetto," Cocofino went on. "He stopped to say good-bye to his colleagues. While he's talking with them, I think, 'Here's my chance before he's gone, and who knows if he'll be back?' I didn't want to ask him right in front of everybody. So, I jump into the cart when he isn't looking and crawl under his bags and boxes. Once away from the noise and confusion, I'd have his full attention when I spoke to him.

"I waited. I didn't make a sound, I hardly dared to breathe. I stayed burrowed into his bundles, reckoning we'd soon be away from town. I kept wondering how I'd convince him to let me stay with him. Before I thought of what I might say, I went to sleep. Next thing I know, the cart stops.

"'All right, Cocofino,' I hear him call. 'I know you're in there. Tumble out and be quick about it.'"

20

Fame and Fortune

"WELL, HE'D CAUGHT ME," Cocofino went on. "I crawled out. What else could I do? And here we are in the middle of a road somewhere. Ferramondo has this big stick, taller than he is, and he's pointing it at me. I'd got myself tangled in one of his cloaks, and I'm stumbling around, stammering, trying to explain why I stowed away.

"'Enough babbling,' he says. 'I get the drift of it. Fame? Fortune? If that's what you're after and you think you'll find it with me, I won't deprive you of the chance.'

"I thanked him a thousand times over. He only grins and tells me to wait and see if I'll really have cause to thank him. I thought, then, we'd climb into the cart and be on our way. But, no, he shakes his head.

"'Pistachio can sit on top of the luggage,' he says. 'You and I go on shank's mare. Aceto has burden enough pulling my cart. Why should I add to it?'

"And that's how it was," Cocofino said. "In all my time with him, we never rode in the cart. Rain or shine, hot or cold, we tramped beside Aceto. I'd never before seen a donkey look grateful, but I swear this one did.

"Now, if you want my opinion"—Cocofino lowered his voice—"I think Ferramondo was grateful, too. Not that he ever let on, but I do believe he was glad to have me along.

"As a magician, he was the best. I'll say that for him. But when he wasn't performing, how he made his way in the world I'll never know. Talk about absentminded? He couldn't keep track of his costumes and equipment. He never knew what tricks he'd do until he was doing them. Why, he'd forget to go to sleep at night. He'd be sitting there, in whatever lodgings I rented for us—he had no idea how to find rooms or dicker with landlords; I did all that—yes, he'd be sitting there, smiling to himself until I nudged him and told him it was past bedtime. Anything practical, he was a baby. He even looked like a baby. An old baby.

"We went from town to town and I'd go on ahead to scout a place where he could perform: an inn, a hall of some sort, a playhouse if there was one. He could never have managed the arrangements himself. Let alone handle the money. I don't believe he could add or subtract. I had to set the admission fees. We always disagreed about that. As often as not, he'd let everybody in free. Such an innocent he was. Can you imagine what he says to me once?

"'Cocofino,' he says, 'if they're poor, they don't have money enough to pay for it. If they're rich, they don't have money enough to pay what it's worth.'

"'Maestro,' I tell him, 'that's not how the world works.'

"'Oh?' He gives me a blinky-eyed look. 'I hadn't noticed.'"

"If you were with him so much," Lidi said, "you must have seen his rope trick."

"Well, as a matter of fact," said Cocofino, "to put it simply: No."

"He never did it?"

"Not exactly. He had the notion of making it a little different. He wanted to teach Pistachio to climb the rope—I didn't understand the ins and outs of all the details, he was closemouthed when it came to that. He and Pistachio would go off somewhere to practice. I never saw what they were up to.

"Another thing, I was busy. At first, I thought he'd teach me some of his tricks. I suppose he would have, if I'd asked. But I had too much else to do. As well as getting him organized, I mended his cloaks, washed his shirts, bought provisions, haggled over prices. I groomed Aceto, combed and brushed Pistachio—we came to be fond of each other—and I was so occupied with my duties, I lost interest in learning tricks. Some other time, I tell myself, when I get 'round to it.

"The daily chores alone were enough to frazzle me. When we camped out, guess who did the cooking and washing up? Once, I was scrubbing the pot and dropped it in the ashes, and had all to do over. I was in a temper, I can tell you. I banged it on the ground and gave it a pretty good whacking.

"'Gently, gently, Cocofino,' he says to me. 'People had to mine the tin, melt it down, and hammer out that pot you're kicking around. There's a bit of their lives in it. You might show a little respect.'

"That vexed me all the more. I muttered something like: 'To a cook pot? What next? I should be polite to sticks and stones?'

"'Why not?' he says. 'It's their world as much as yours. Look at them up close; they have their own personality. I've met any number of perfectly delightful rocks and logs.'

"I'd never heard such silliness. But, you know, it stuck in my mind. I started being pleasant and cordial to ferns, pinecones, frogs, earthworms—though I felt like a fool doing it.

"Then, one day, what does he do? He's talking to Aceto as if that jackass could answer him. 'I'll miss your company,' he says, 'but fair is fair. You've worked long and hard, old friend. It's time you're free to enjoy yourself. So, off you go.'

"And he unhitches Aceto, pats him on the head, and sends him galloping into the fields, kicking up his heels, frisky as a colt.

"'But—maestro,' I say to him, 'what have you done? Who's to pull the cart?'

"'You and I,' he says. 'If an elderly donkey can do it, so can we.'

"'He was wrong. We set ourselves between the shafts and

hauled away. We couldn't manage. The cart kept going off the road, and finally tipped over into a ditch. It didn't bother him at all. 'Leave it there. Someone's bound to come along and find some use for it. We'll carry the luggage.'

"From then on, that's what we did. With Pistachio trotting alongside, we carried those bags on our back. I got used to it, after a time. I did, once in a while, say to myself, 'Cocofino, my boy, if this is fame and fortune, it's giving you the lumbago.' But I was too busy to think on it much.

"Around that time, Ferramondo got himself in a bad piece of trouble." Cocofino paused a moment and sadly shook his head. "Not that I blame him; he was just being his usual self, such an innocent old baby. I wish he'd known better.

"We were in the Duchy of Frascati then, having dinner at an inn, when a fine carriage and pair of horses roll up. Out steps a hoity-toity lackey dripping with gold braid. He tells Ferramondo that his master, Duke Orsino, desires—which means 'commands'—his presence to entertain a few party guests.

"Ferramondo shrugs and says he'll be glad to oblige, since he has nothing better to do at the moment. He was cool and calm about performing for the nobility, but I'm thinking: 'Aha! Here's my start on fame and fortune.'

"It surprised me he didn't take any equipment with him, only that big staff of his. And Pistachio, of course. We're whisked away into the countryside to the duke's villa. What a place it was! Nearest thing to a palace I'd ever seen. A couple of flunkeys usher us into the grand salon; and there's the duke himself, all frilled out in evening clothes, and his few guests, maybe sixty or seventy.

"'Now, then, Signor Magician,' says the duke, a fellow who looks as if he never met a meal he didn't like. 'This rope trick you do. Quite amusing, I'm told. So, get on with it and let's see what you have to show us.'

"'Sorry to tell you, Orsino, I'm not prepared to do it,' says Ferramondo—at which, the duke begins to scowl. 'But I'll be happy to offer another diversion. I propose to turn your most valuable possession into something of still greater value.'

"'Will you, indeed?' says the duke. His eyebrows go up and I can see Ferramondo has caught a fish. 'Well, well, that should be more amusing than a piece of old rope. Most valuable possession? Hard to choose which one.'

"The duke thinks it over awhile. Then he whispers to one of the flunkeys, who hurries off and fetches a velvet-covered jewel box.

"'Does this suit you, Signor Magician?' The duke lifts the lid and hands Ferramondo a pearl the size of a pigeon's egg. I'd never seen anything so grand; I also wonder what kind of giant oyster could have made it. 'I don't need to tell you what it cost me.'

"'That's right. You don't,' says Ferramondo. 'But I gather you prize it, since you keep it locked away in your strong room, and, I'd guess, hardly ever lay eyes on it.'

"'Of course not,' says Orsino. 'Why would I? I know it's there. No one has anything like it. It's a treasure.'

"'Adequate,' says Ferramondo. 'It will serve the purpose.'

"With that, he sets the pearl on the floor and whacks it with the tip of his staff until all that's left is a pile of grit.

"The ladies gasp as if their own jewels were being ground up; the gentlemen stare, horrified. Orsino yawns.

"'You'll have to do better than that,' he says. 'I expected something a touch more amusing. Come, now, I've seen second-rate conjurers do that same tired old trick.

"'I know the routine,' Orsino goes on. 'You're going to spread a handkerchief over that heap of dust. Then you'll waggle your stick, mumble some sort of abracadabra, and give my pearl back safe and sound.'

"'No,' says Ferramondo."

21

The Condottieri

"'NO?' ORSINO FROWNS. 'What do you mean?'

"'Just that,' says Ferramondo. 'No.'

"'This trick doesn't please me,' says the duke. 'Give back the pearl and do something entertaining.'

"'I can't,' says Ferramondo. 'The pearl's gone. As a pearl, that is. It's still there, but in a different way.'

"I feel my stomach sink to my ankles," Cocofino continued. "Orsino's face turns the color of undercooked beef. Ferramondo bends down and sweeps the dust into his palm.

"'I promised I'd turn it into something more valuable,' he says while Orsino twitches and grinds his teeth. 'And so I will. The trick's not over.'

"Orsino relaxes a little, but still he looks not very comfortable. Ferramondo goes on.

"'Dig a hole in your garden. Sprinkle the dust into it. Then plant a fig-tree branch—'

"'Oho!' Orsino claps his hands. 'Now I see what you're up to. A fig tree's going to spring up in the twinkling of an eye, loaded with ripe figs and a pearl in every one. Bravo!'"

"'Even better,' says Ferramondo.

"'There's more?' says the duke. 'Of course! You live up to your reputation. It grows golden apples? Diamonds big as walnuts—?'

"'Figs,' Ferramondo says. 'That's what a fig tree does, and in its own good time. In fact, one day you'll have so many figs you'll be glad to give them away. It will bear fruit for generations to come. You might contemplate giving away branches so other people can grow their own fig trees, and others after them. Tell me, Orsino, in all honesty: Isn't that more valuable than an oversized pearl?'

"Orsino doesn't answer. The whole room goes dead silent," Cocofino went on. "All I can do is hold my head and think: Oh, Ferramondo, you innocent baby, what have you done now?'

"Orsino finally smiles—with his mouth but not the rest of his face.

"'You're a witty fellow,' he says. 'I enjoy a good joke as long as it's not at my expense. So now I have a little joke for you.

"'There's a dungeon here, from the days of my great-grandfather. I haven't had occasion to use it—so far. I'm locking you in it, and your cat. You stay until the tree bears fruit. We'll see, then, who has the last laugh.'

"Orsino snaps his fingers and in come a couple of burly retainers. I'm out of my wits, beside myself, I don't know what to do. Except ask to be locked up in the dungeon, too, so I can look after him.

"'Don't worry,' Ferramondo says to me. 'Pistachio and I will be glad for the chance to rest in quiet contemplation. Go home. Do as I tell you. Live your life. You'll find fame and fortune, I promise.

"'But, Cocofino'—and he gives me a little smile and a slantwise look—'be sure you recognize them when you find them.'

"I had to do what he ordered, no arguing with him. I wasn't happy to leave, but I go back to the Burghetto. And there I am, at loose ends as before.

"By lucky coincidence, the town baker needed an apprentice and he hired me. And, do you know it turned out I had a knack for the pastry trade. It suited me; I adored making cakes and pies. I got better and better at it. And, best yet, I fell in love with the baker's daughter—and we married.

"When the baker gets too old to handle a rolling pin, he turns the business over to me. My pastries—famous! Everybody wants them, I'm sold out before the day's done. My jam tarts, those rascals, practically walk out of the shop. Talk about good fortune? Just look at my beautiful wife and our young ones. Nearly a baker's dozen, you might say."

"I'm glad for you," Lidi said. "You never saw Ferramondo again?"

"No, more's the pity," said Cocofino. "For all I know, he could still be in Orsino's dungeon. Somehow, I doubt it. Every so often, a wandering juggler or some other artiste passes through here and claims he's seen him since then."

"Why did Mercurio think he was dead?"

"Well, there was a rumor that he taught Pistachio to do the rope trick with him. One day, the story goes, Pistachio climbed up, Ferramondo after him, and they both disappeared. People couldn't believe their eyes; they talked about it for weeks. But I put no stock in it."

One of the youngsters came with a bag of pastries for Daniella. Lidi stood up. "Nothing more that can help us?"

"I wish there were. Oh, my goodness!" Cocofino smacked his forehead. "The apple puffs! I nearly forgot. They need a word of cheer. They sulk if I neglect them. A pleasure talking with you—but, a busy day, you understand. Excuse me."

"By all means," Jericho said. "While you're at it, give them my warmest regards."

"What next?" Julian said after they left the pastry shop.

"I don't know," Lidi said. "I don't know what to make of it. Nobody agrees on much of anything about Ferramondo, but he sounds more and more surprising, even apart from his rope trick. I have to see him for myself. If what Cocofino tells me is true—but I wonder if what anybody tells me is true—"

"The wild-goose chase gets wilder," Jericho grumbled. "All chase and no goose."

Daniella, on the wagon bench, dipped into the sack of pastries. Julian drew Lidi aside.

"What about the Added Attraction?" he asked. "Sometimes she says things as if she already knew what was going to happen. Could she tell you?"

"I did ask her, once," Lidi said. "She only came out with a lot of nonsense. I don't understand what goes on inside her head. I don't think she does either. Things must drift into her mind in bits and pieces; she can't control them. She may, when she gets older. Or, whatever it is she has, she might lose it altogether, like baby teeth. Most of the time, when she isn't seeing things, she's just a happy little girl.

"I hoped she might help me," Lidi added. "She wasn't able to."

"Ask her again," Julian said. "Why not? It's all you have left."

Lidi nodded. "I'll try once more. I'll talk to her later, quietly. Right now I only want to go away. There's nothing for us here."

For the first time, then, she said what she had been unwilling even to think:

"Maybe there's nothing for us anywhere."

Perched on the bench, the Added Attraction busily licked cake crumbs from her fingers.

————

Shadows were trickling over the hillside by the time the wagons reached the road again. Lidi could barely see the town
high above. She halted soon after that. There was no point
going farther in the deepening twilight. She had no heart for
it, in any case.

Julian unhitched the draft horses and tethered them near
the poplar trees along with the stolen mount. While Jericho
made the cook fire, Lidi took Daniella aside and sat her
down just beyond the property wagon.

"Let's talk a minute." Lidi took the child's hand. "Listen
to me. Carefully. I have to decide what we're going to do."

"Eat dinner," Daniella said.

"After that. Tomorrow. I don't know where to go next. I
need you to help me. For real, this time."

Daniella tried to pull away. Lidi put an arm around her
shoulders.

"It's important," Lidi insisted. "Do you see anything ahead
for us? Anything at all? Try hard. Can you tell me . . . ?"

Daniella gave the cry of a small, wounded animal. Then,
suddenly, she began to sob. Her body shook as she gasped
for breath. Her lips moved, trying to shape words, but there
was only the sobbing.

Lidi, frightened, held her and rocked her back and forth,
stroking her hair, whispering it was all right, it was all right.
Daniella hid her face against Lidi's breast. The heaving and
choking eased a little. Lidi held her until the child was quiet.

Daniella, at last, snuffled and wiped her nose on her
sleeve. "I'm hungry."

"Go eat," Lidi said.

She sat, her face in her hands. A horse whickered. It was not one of her animals; the sound had come from beyond the trees. She raised her head. A long shadow slid out of the hedges.

She jumped to her feet. A man with a grimy bandanna knotted around his head took a pace toward her. He pointed a musket.

Lidi's chin went up. She was in no mood to be robbed or murdered. "What do you want?"

"Whatever you've got."

"Take my best advice," Lidi said. "Rob somebody else."

The man hesitated, his musket still leveled at her. Some others, four or five, came out of the bushes behind him. As best she could see, they were young, roughly dressed. One of them led the horse she heard whickering.

"So? Now?" Lidi stepped closer, calculating her chances of wresting away the gun. "You're going to shoot me? I don't recommend it."

"We don't shoot women," he said.

"You don't shoot anybody here."

Julian had come up beside her. He shouted something and threw himself at the intruder. Instead of grappling with the man, Julian flung his arms around him.

"Matteo!" Julian burst out laughing and slapped him on the back. The others drew closer. An instant later, they were tousling one another's hair, giving one another friendly punches on the arms, and carrying on like a bunch of boys.

Lidi, expecting a fight, found herself in the midst of what looked like some kind of family reunion.

"From Malvento," Julian said to her. "Matteo. And here's Beppo. And Sandro—"

"You're his girl?" The young man called Matteo bobbed his head at Lidi. "Forgive the mistake. How could I know? Anyhow, I swear I wouldn't have shot you."

"I'm relieved to hear that," Lidi said.

"What's this now?" Julian said. "What are you boys up to? Come, come." He hurried on, leading Matteo and his friends to the wagons. Daniella, dinner plate in hand, smiled calmly at the new arrivals.

"Expect me to feed them?" Jericho muttered when Julian began the introductions again. "They'll eat beans. That's it."

"We ran off. Quit the estate," Matteo said as Julian pressed him with a dozen questions at once. "No more of that hellhole." He put a hand on Julian's arm. "Listen, *amico,* sad news, but I have to tell you. Your aunt Bella— never the same after Renzo was killed. She died a month after you left. I'm sorry. A shame."

"A shame, yes." Julian's face hardened. "And the Baboon?"

"Alive and well."

"Good," Julian said. "I want him to stay that way. He's mine."

"Ours, too," Matteo said. "We have our own scores to settle. There's more bad news. The *marchese*'s come back."

"Himself? On the estate?" Julian frowned. "He's never been there before. Nobody's ever laid eyes on him."

"Well, he's there now," Matteo said. "He's living high style in the mansion house. He's come to take charge. Personally. The landholding isn't bringing in enough profit. It's run too slack to suit him. He means to tighten things up." Matteo made a sour face. "Any tighter, you'll see our backsides through our breeches.

"You thought it was bad? Worse." Matteo spat. "He's got the Baboon squeezing the blood out of us, and putting the stick about if anyone falls short. Poor harvest? Miss payment on a debt? He'll pull down our houses and turn us into beggars. Damn the Baboon and the *marchese* twice over.

"They pushed us past bearing. One day, I say to my boys here, '*Ragazzi,* I'm for the open road. Who's with me? If we're going to starve, we can starve nicely on our own.'"

"And so," Jericho said, "instead of the begging profession, you went into the robbery trade."

"No, no! Please!" Matteo waved his arms in protest. "Not robbers. We're *condottieri*. Like the olden days. We'll fight for the tenantry and the smallholders wherever they are. They need us to protect them—"

"If I understand it right," put in Jericho, "the old *condottieri* ended up serving themselves very well. They kept it neat and simple. They took everything. I guess that's protection of a sort."

"We won't do that. Not us," Matteo said earnestly. "We're on the side of the *cafoni*. We're *cafoni* ourselves. Simple justice is all we want," he added. "Once we get a few more strong fellows to join us, that's the end of brutes like the Baboon and his master.

"And you, *amico*." Matteo turned admiringly to Julian. "You're quite the famous hero. They talk about you all over the province. All over Campania, I wouldn't be surprised. How you faced up to the Baboon, defied him, tore his whip out of his hands and beat him with it. Saved Renzo's life. Rallied the *cafoni,* marched on the mansion house—"

"Not exactly like that," Julian said. "The Baboon? He flogged me till I bawled like a baby. Renzo's the one who saved *my* life. You know it, you were there. Not much of a rally. Not much of a march. Not much of a hero."

"But close enough." Matteo pointed at the wagons. "And what's all this? You'll have some good tales for us."

"Leave them to themselves." Jericho motioned for Lidi and Daniella to draw away from the cook fire. "They have a lot of catching up to do."

Lidi glanced back at Julian and the others, high-spirited now, laughing, gossiping about people she never heard of. They were his old friends, grown up together. A part of his life she could never share.

"That fellow Matteo," Jericho was saying. "He's young, he's eager, and he has a gun. That makes for interesting consequences."

After a while, Julian came alone to them. "They're leaving now," he said. "The *carabinieri*'s muskets. Matteo would be glad to have them."

"You stole them. Do as you please." Jericho went to fetch the weapons from the tent wagon.

"The horse?" Julian asked Lidi.

"Stolen, too," she said. "It's yours to give. What else do they want?"

Julian stood awkwardly for some moments. He took a step closer to her:

"Me," he said. "I'm going with them."

22

A Lost Purse

HE LEFT WITH THE REST OF THEM. She did not wait to see him go. For a time, she was unsure what they had said to each other. She knew she had not cried, not in front of him, not so he could see. After she had flung herself away and run into the wagon, some of it came back to her.

"Don't you see? Don't you see?" he kept saying. "I have to do this."

He was speaking quickly, as if he needed to let the words out all at once. He told her again and again that they needed him, it would bring others to join if he was with them. They would go after the Baboon. He meant to settle it, be done with it once and for all. A matter of principle.

She wanted to hear none of that.

"A first-of-May," she said. "Here in the spring, gone in the autumn. I always knew it," she said, which was not altogether true.

She had, during this, tried to make Daniella go somewhere else. The child stood, refusing to move, looking at him, an unreadable expression on her face, her lips forming a silent *I knew*.

At one point, Lidi remembered, she called him a liar. She reminded him of the time she heard him say he never wanted to leave her. It was a lie. As if that made any difference now.

"I don't want to leave you. Never wanted to," he said. "I have to."

Jericho, by then, had come with the muskets. No one needed to explain. He understood immediately. He threw the muskets to the ground. He said angry things to Julian. Lidi left the two of them and went into the wagon. Still in her clothes, she lay down on the cot. She did not hear Daniella come in.

She slept heavily, as if she had been stunned, and woke exhausted. It was a cool, misty morning. Dew beaded the grass. Daniella was busy finishing breakfast. Jericho had already hitched up the draft horses. All as usual, nothing out of the ordinary. Except he was not there.

"I should have taken him apart, piece by piece," Jericho said. "I didn't even hit him. Damn him. I'd come to like him."

"I loved him," Lidi said.

"I know." Jericho put an arm around her. "It's all right. For the best."

Lidi nodded. She said no more about it. She would have to decide what next to do. There was nothing of any use that she could do. Jericho talked about the weather. Winter in the south was milder than winter in the north, but it would still be raw, cold rains, nasty traveling, small audiences.

Why, she thought, is he talking about weather? The weather did not interest her.

"The seacoast is warmer," he went on. "Pleasant there, so I hear."

She understood. "Pompadoro?"

"We just might run into him," Jericho said. "Easy enough to find him if you wanted. In fact, he'd be hard to miss."

"Are we going to see the piggies now?" Daniella said.

"You'd like that?" Lidi said.

Daniella brightened. "I always like to see the piggies."

———

The sun came out later and burned away the mist. In the vineyards, men, women, and children picked bunches of fat black grapes and heaped them in baskets. A little farther, Lidi noticed a woman sitting on a bundle, her head in her hands. As Lidi drove closer, the woman looked up. Her face was sun-blistered, her brow wrinkled; she was very thin.

Lidi halted the wagon. The woman stared at her, saying nothing. Lidi climbed down. "Are you all right?"

"I will be," the woman said. "Once I'm home. Not far now."

"Do you want to ride with us awhile?" Lidi saw that her shoes were cracked and split, practically falling off her feet.

The bundle seemed to be mainly rags. The woman got up stiffly.

"I can't pay," she said.

"I didn't ask you to. Where are you going?"

The woman motioned with her head. "Malvento."

Lidi felt a twinge in her heart. His town. "Tell me how to find it," she said, after a moment. "We can take you there."

The woman had been studying the lettering on the side of the wagon. "You're Princess Lidi? I remember—yes, I saw you once. Months ago, it must have been. I've lost track of the time."

Daniella hopped down to look curiously at her. "I'm the Added Attraction."

"My name is Antonia. And what a lovely child you are." She smiled and turned to Lidi. "Your little girl?"

"In a manner of speaking," Lidi said. "But—where did you see us?"

The woman named a town Lidi did not recognize. It could have been any one of the dozen she had passed through.

"I lived there—until I had to leave," Antonia said. "I was born and raised in Malvento. I'm going to my sister's house. We've hardly seen each other since we were girls together. But we were close in those days. I know she'll take me in."

"How did you come this far?"

"I walked," Antonia said. "As I had made up my mind to do."

"Have you eaten? Do you want something?"

"If you have food to spare. I'm not a beggar," Antonia quickly added. "That *malandrino,* that villain—he'd have liked nothing better than seeing me beg for scraps. I wouldn't give him the satisfaction—"

Antonia broke off as Jericho came to see why they had halted. Lidi repeated what she had offered to do.

"We can turn off and take her to Malvento. It won't be much out of our way."

"When do we see the piggies?" Daniella put in.

"Soon," Lidi said. Jericho went to bring what was left of their meal. Daniella turned her attention to Antonia.

"What about the *malandrino*? What did he do to you?"

"Hush," Lidi said. "It's rude to pry."

"I'm not prying," Daniella said. "I'm asking."

"I can tell you," Antonia said. "I make no secret of it. What happened, happened. I can't change it. I should have been more careful, I blame only myself.

"My husband died a year ago," she went on. "Dear man, he was a good tailor with a bad head for business. I don't reproach him—it's the way he was. A loving man, we were happy together. When he died, he left me with fond memories—and heavy debts.

"The money had to be repaid, somehow or other. I went to work as a laundress. I scrimped to put aside all I could from what I earned. I spent next to nothing on food or heat. In time, I saved enough to pay back every penny.

"The morning when the debts were due, I set off for the moneylender's countinghouse, glad to be free of that skinflint for good and all. I carried my basket of laundry to deliver to my customers along the way. I had my purse in my apron pocket.

"He's sitting there at his table, with his cash boxes and ledgers. 'I've come to settle with you,' I tell him. 'Payment in full, I'm free and clear.'

"I reach for my purse. My pocket's empty. My head spins, I can't believe it. I look again and again, turn my apron inside out, search through the basket to see if I had, by accident, put it among the laundry. Nothing. Had some thief picked my pocket? Had the purse fallen in the street and I never noticed? I knew I had it with me when I left my house. But—now?

"'Come, come, signora,' he says, drumming his fingers on the table. 'My time is money and your time is up. Your mortgage on your house, the lien on your belongings, all itemized and noted down. Here's the paper you signed. And the date promised, which is today. Today, signora. Now. Not a moment later.'

"I pleaded with him to give me time to look for my purse, mislaid, misplaced somewhere. If I had dropped it along the way, I could retrace my steps and try to find it.

"'Find money lying in the street? Not likely,' he scoffs. 'How do I know you're not making up some flimsy lie and you never had it in the first place? You'll not cheat me out of what you owe. Either you have the money or you don't. Hand it over this minute or suffer the consequences. Why should I lose my honest profit because of your carelessness?'

"Nothing would move him. Oh, he had a heart of stone,

that one. Within the hour, he called the law on me. He turned me out of my home, seized my household goods, and left me a pauper.

"I think he'd have relished seeing me beg on the streets, shamed in front of all the town. I wouldn't give him that pleasure. I set off on foot for Malvento. And here I am, as you see me.

"I'll not forget the last thing he said," Antonia went on. 'Let this be an example to anyone who thinks they can get the better of Scabbia.'"

"Scabbia?" Lidi caught her breath. "That disgusting ferret—"

"It sounds as if you know him," Antonia said.

"All too well. Antonia, you did lose your purse in the street. Scabbia's the one who found it."

"He had my money? And ruined me nonetheless?" cried Antonia. "How do you know this?"

"We were performing in your town," Lidi began. "Scabbia came that night—"

"To see the Added Attraction," Daniella put in.

"He insisted on having his fortune told," Lidi said. "Daniella put him off with a pack of nonsense—she does that when she's tired and can't think of anything better. She told him money would come into his hands, just to get rid of him. He came back again, sure the prophecy was true. He'd found a purse lying in the street. Antonia, it could only have been yours. He still wasn't satisfied. He wanted more from Daniella. A long story I'll tell you later."

Lidi broke off as Jericho urged her to start for Malvento.

"If we get a move on, we'll have the rest of the day to travel. We can be well on our way to the seacoast. If that's what you want."

"I don't know. I need time to think," Lidi said, meaning she needed time to forget. "What to do about Ferramondo—"

Antonia had picked up her bundle and stepped toward the wagon. She stopped suddenly. "Ferramondo?"

"Another long story," Lidi said. "But—you've heard of him?"

"He saved my life," Antonia said.

23

Malvento

"FERRAMONDO?" LIDI HAD BARELY begun to absorb the idea that Scabbia had found the purse and turned Antonia penniless; and that Daniella—and herself, as well—had some part in it. For the moment, she put away the idea, along with others she preferred not to think about. "What happened? When?"

"Ah, that was years ago," Antonia said. "In Malvento. My sister and I—"

"We can't lose daylight," Jericho broke in. "When we cross into Ardita Vecchia, we'll have border guards to deal with, and who knows what kind of mess they'll make for us."

Antonia laughed for the first time. "Did I grow up in these parts for nothing? We learn at our mother's knee how to get around border guards and toll collectors. There are half a dozen bypasses, I remember every one of them." She gave Lidi a pitying smile. "Only outlanders pay attention to guard posts."

"It's a crazy country," Jericho said. "I almost forgot."

To satisfy Jericho's impatience, Lidi helped Antonia climb aboard with her bundle. Daniella sat between them while Lidi followed her passenger's directions.

"It was long ago," Antonia began again. "My sister Bettina and I were only half-grown girls. She was two years older, but I was the bigger scamp.

"Malvento's not much of a market town. Between us, Bettina and I had used up whatever chances for mischief we could find. We'd run out of scrapes to get into. Until we could think of new ones, we had the notion of climbing into the hills beyond town. We'd never gone all the way up. We'd been forbidden, warned to stay away. Because of the ogre."

"You had an ogre in the neighborhood?" Lidi said. "Not really—"

"So we'd always been told. Some of the old folks claimed it was the ghost of a wicked *condottiere* who roamed the hills looking for disobedient young girls to snatch away. Most others agreed it was a hungry monster who ate people for dinner.

"Bettina and I talked a lot about the ogre. We tried to imagine what he looked like. Maybe like the mean old Marchese di Malvento—except no one had ever seen him, so that didn't help us. We thought of the fairy tales our mother used to tell. He'd have big eyes to see people at a distance, a big nose to sniff them out if they tried to hide, and big ears to hear them. Big teeth, of course, to chew people up; and a belly big enough to digest them. Putting all that together, we decided our ogre—we'd come to think of him as 'our' ogre—had to look like Santino, who spent most of his days in the tavern.

"We kept daring each other to go into the hills. And at last we did. Our mother had gone out on errands and wouldn't be back for hours. It was warm and sunny, just the kind of afternoon to hunt for our ogre, though we weren't sure what we'd do once we found him.

"We left our chores undone, slipped out of the house, and dodged our way past the edge of town. We were a little frightened; excited as well." Antonia's eyes sparkled with recollections of old mischief. "We knew we were being naughty, which made it all the better.

"We climbed as high as we could," she went on, "and never got a glimpse of our ogre. We were disappointed, of course, and maybe relieved. Still, it was good enough to have sneaked off as we were forbidden to do. We picked wildflowers and put them in our hair. We lurked behind bushes and jumped out to scare each other. We played hide-and-seek—Bettina always found me right away, so this time I ran off farther than I'd ever gone. I meant to scramble along a stony shelf above a dry stream bed and circle around behind her.

"What happened—I'm not exactly sure," Antonia said. "I know I missed my footing and went tumbling down. I remember banging my head on a rock as I landed. When I opened my eyes again, I'd been hauled onto the bank, my head pounding and going 'round in circles. A man was kneeling beside me on the grass. I asked him:

"'Are you the ogre?'"

"'Not as far as I know,'" he said.

"He had on a goatskin jacket and a herdsman's leather breeches. When I had a better look at him, my head danced around more than ever, but not from being hit on a rock. He was the handsomest young man I'd ever seen."

Antonia actually blushed as she went on. "Oh, indeed he was. Broad-shouldered, with the beginnings of a reddish beard, and eyes so bright they crackled." She smiled distantly. "I can tell you I fell in love with him then and there.

"He picks me up as if I weighed nothing and carries me in his arms to a cart track—I was glad, because my knees would have wobbled so much I never could have walked.

"We went a good ways up into the hills to a sort of hut built against the slope, with a dooryard of packed earth. I saw a cart, and a donkey browsing nearby. Inside, he sat me down on a bench; the room was cool and quiet, with boxes and bags all neatly stored, a table, a straw mattress—I wasn't paying much attention to furniture, for I hardly took my eyes off him. He got a basin of water and a cloth to make a compress for the lump on my head, which felt bigger than my fist; not that I cared about that.

"I said that I didn't think anyone—except the ogre—lived in the hills.

"'I do, from time to time,' he said. 'When I get tired of traveling. My name's Ferramondo. I'm a magician by trade.'

"I had never seen a magic show. My uncle did, once at a country fair, and never stopped talking about it. I asked Ferramondo if he'd do a trick for me.

"He only laughed. 'You, child, have more magic in you than I'll ever have. The best trick is for you to get home as fast as you can.'

"When he judged I was steady enough to walk, he led me out to the trail and pointed me toward Malvento. I hung back, dawdling and shuffling my feet. I didn't want to leave; I asked him if I could stay a while longer.

"'You'll find me again,' he said. 'Be sure of that.'

"It was dark when I got home. Bettina was already there; she'd given up looking for me. My mother and father were frantic, getting ready to call the constables and send out a search party. When I walked through the door, they carried on worse than before, my father yelling at me, my mother bursting into tears. They hugged me, scolded me, petted me, furious and overjoyed at the same time.

"After they calmed down a little, I told them what happened and showed them the lump on my head. They didn't believe a word. Oh, they agreed I'd fallen down and had the wits knocked out of me. Ferramondo? They insisted I dreamed the whole thing while I was unconscious. Either that or I was making it all up.

"They kept at me and at me, telling me it was nonsense, nobody lived in the hills, least of all a wandering magician. I gave up trying to make them believe me, and that was the end of that."

"You never went back?"

"No. First, my mother punished Bettina and me by locking us inside the house for a long time; and, from then on, she kept an eye on me like a hen with one chick. I hardly had a chance to slip away and my chores kept me busy. Not that I forgot Ferramondo; he was always in the back of my mind. But, as I grew a couple of years older, I came halfway to believe I did imagine it.

"Later, I had other things to think about. Young men began calling on Bettina and me, no shortage of suitors for either of us. Bettina soon got married. I didn't, though I was expected to. My mother told me I was too picky, I'd better hurry up and choose a husband.

"I couldn't," Antonia went on. "I just couldn't bring myself to do it. My suitors were nice enough, but I turned them all down. You see, I was looking for someone who'd make me feel the way I felt the day I met Ferramondo. None of them did.

"The last one who came courting—my mother and sister rolled their eyes, giggled, and whispered behind their hands. He was shy, and stammering, tripping over his own feet, with no prospects for much of anything. In fact, he was leaving Malvento, sure he could set himself up as a tailor and do better somewhere else.

"My sister thought he was the silliest person she'd ever seen. But as soon as I set eyes on him, I lost my heart, just as with Ferramondo. I knew he was the one for me. And so I married him and was never happier.

"I remembered Ferramondo saying 'You'll find me again.' In a way, I did."

"You were lucky," Lidi said. "I wish—never mind, it makes no difference. What I'm thinking—you didn't dream. It really happened. Antonia, could you find that place in the hills?"

Antonia smiled. "Blindfolded and in my sleep."

"Take me there," Lidi said.

———————

They pulled up in a clearing on the outskirts of Malvento. Lidi repeated Antonia's account to Jericho.

"We'll go into the hills tomorrow," she said. "I want to see that hut. I can't hope Ferramondo's there. But—who knows? There might be some clue, something, anything that could help, at least give me an idea. I certainly don't have one now."

"If there isn't?"

"Then it's over," Lidi said. "One more chance. My last. If there's nothing useful—we turn back and go to the seacoast. Pompadoro said he'd be glad to have us join him; he didn't want us to leave in the first place. Ferramondo? The rope trick? That's the end of it. No more wild-goose chase."

"Your decision," Jericho said. "I don't know whether to be glad or sorry."

"Take your choice," Lidi said.

———————

She left Jericho at the tent wagon. She would take the property wagon and drive Antonia to her sister's house and be back before the end of the day. Next morning, then, they would pass through town, pick up Antonia to guide them into the hills. If the trail was too steep, they would park the wagons and go the rest of the way on foot.

Daniella coaxed and fussed until Lidi let her come along. The Added Attraction chattered happily with Antonia. Lidi was silent; one thing was still on her mind, one thing she understood she had to do.

"The purse you lost," she said at last to Antonia as they jogged into Malvento. "Do you remember how much was in it?"

"Yes, to the penny," Antonia said. "How could I forget? It all went into Scabbia's pocket."

She was startled when Antonia told the sum. It was exactly what Lidi had in her purse.

She handed the money to Antonia. "I want you to take this. What you lost, you have back again."

"No, no," Antonia said. "None of it was your fault. Only coincidence—"

"If Daniella hadn't told Scabbia's fortune," Lidi said, "I can't guess how things would have turned out. If and if and if. Coincidence? It doesn't matter. We were tangled up in it one way or another. Threads on a loom, as someone said to me."

Antonia, reluctant but grateful, at last took what Lidi offered. "Good," Lidi said. "What happened to you was wrong. I have a chance to set it right. The only thing I've been able to set right."

Following Antonia's directions, she pulled up in front of a plaster-walled house near the market square. She shook her head when Antonia urged her to come inside and meet Bettina.

"Tomorrow," Lidi said, "when we pick you up. You and your sister have a lot to talk about. I don't want to intrude."

The fact was she had no heart for happy reunions. Once Antonia stepped through the door and Lidi heard the joyful commotion, she turned back to the square. Malvento was like other towns she had passed through and forgotten, different only because it was his town. She wondered how often he had come here, seeing the same shabby storefronts, the same narrow streets that she saw now. She looked into the faces of the passers-by. Had he known them? He. She still could not say his name even in her thoughts.

He told her, the day they first met, no magic show had ever come to Malvento. As she drove back through the square, the townsfolk saw the bright lettering PRINCESS LIDI'S MAGICAL MYSTIFICATIONS. They pressed closer, clutching at the horse's bridle, calling out for her to do some tricks. Daniella, delighted by so much attention, blew kisses.

"No performance," Lidi told her. She realized, then, that she had emptied her purse for Antonia. Not that Jericho would reproach her; he would know she had done the right thing. At worst, he would give her a long-suffering look if she came back empty-handed.

"All right," she said, before Daniella had a chance to wheedle her into it. "A few tricks, earn some money, and we go."

She went to get a couple of small items from the wagon. When she came out, the Added Attraction was sitting on the step. A line had already formed, the spectators' interest divided between Daniella's fortune-telling and Lidi's hastily put together program.

She did nothing out of the ordinary. Some card tricks; a bouquet of paper flowers that suddenly appeared in her hands and vanished again—it half embarrassed her to do such easy illusions. The faces of the onlookers lit up as if they had been starved for wonders. Daniella was doing such a brisk business Lidi had to pull her away from the crowd.

It was nightfall by the time she drove back to the clearing. She would tell Jericho about the money later. She wanted, now, only to be by herself. Too tired to pack away her gear, she left it where she dropped it. She fell on the cot and tried to think of nothing.

Daniella was fast asleep when Lidi woke again. Restless, she left the wagon and paced deeper into the fringe of trees. She shivered, not from the cold.

He was there.

She knew it even before she heard his voice. She did not turn to look at him.

"What more do you want?" she said. "You took it all. Or did you forget something?"

"I forgot how much I wanted to be with you."

"You have a bad memory," Lidi said. "Go away. Don't touch me," she said, which was not what she meant.

He had stepped in front of her. He held out the paper bouquet Lidi had dropped. "I looked for you in the wagon."

"Why did you come back? You have other things to do."

"Only one," he said. "To be here."

"So you brought me paper flowers. That sets everything right?"

"I wanted to bring you something." He handed her the bouquet. "It was all I could find."

"A matter of principle?" Lidi said.

"I gave up the hero business," he said. "I was never a hero to begin with. Matteo's better at it than I am. He likes it."

"How do I know you'll stay? This time?"

"I set out to kill a man," he said. "Now it doesn't matter. He's not important. I found out something."

"Which is?"

"Very simple. I found out I loved you more than I hated him."

"You gave the right answer."

She suddenly noticed how green and fresh the leaves had become in her hand, and the fragrance from the living flowers.

"Julian—" she cried. "Look—"

A blast of heat struck her like a fist. She heard Daniella scream. From the clearing, flames shot into the night sky.

The wagons were burning.

24

The Marchese

"DANIELLA! JERICHO!"

Lidi ran to the clearing. The horses had broken their tether and bolted into the woods. The tent wagon was burning beyond hope; the rolls of canvas only fed the blaze. Julian sped past her through the shattered door of the property wagon. Lidi plunged after him, choking in the clouds of smoke. Fire had swallowed most of the floorboards, the roof sagged and showered sparks. The alcove where she stored her tricks and equipment was a furnace.

"Nobody here. Get out." Julian had to force her from the collapsing ruins. She stumbled, gasping, into the clearing. The roar of the flames deafened her. She could scarcely breathe, the fire still burned in her lungs.

"Gone. Both." Julian searched around the blazing skeletons of the wagons. She saw him stop suddenly. A figure sprawled near the underbrush.

She was at his side in an instant. "Jericho!"

The canvasmaster lay full-length on his back, one arm outstretched. His face was bloody. She and Julian helped him sit up. He had been badly beaten; anyone but Jericho would have been more dead than alive. With Lidi and Julian on either side, he got unsteadily to his feet.

"They were on horses. Too many for me," Jericho said between clenched teeth.

"Daniella?" Lidi cried. "Daniella?"

"Damn them!" Jericho burst out. "They took her."

"Who?" Lidi pressed. "Where did they go?"

"Don't know." Jericho shook his battered head. "I think I got one of them."

"You did." Julian caught sight of a man lying awkwardly near the bushes. He went and prodded him with the toe of his boot. The man groaned.

"Still breathing," Julian said.

"Too bad," Jericho said.

Julian narrowed his eyes, then seized the man by the shirtfront. "I know him," he called. "Muzio. One of the Baboon's boys."

Julian shook him furiously; the man's head lolled back and forth. When his eyelids twitched open, he tried to squirm away.

"Look at me." Julian locked a hand around Muzio's throat. "Where's the girl?"

Muzio gaped at him. "You?"

"The girl!" Julian shouted. "Where?"

Muzio made choking noises. Julian would have struck him across the face, but Jericho put a hand on his arm.

"Allow me. A personal favor." He thrust out his big jaw and bent close to Muzio. "Signor Muzio, is it? I'm happy to make your acquaintance. You won't be happy to make mine." He pulled Muzio up by the hair. "You understand what I'm talking about."

"He can be very energetic," Julian said.

"Not me, not me," Muzio blurted. "None of it my idea. I only did what they told me. The Baboon—he wanted to burn your wagons. He took the girl to the estate—"

"I enjoyed our little chat," Jericho said. "Now you'll kindly show us the way."

"No need," Julian said. "I know how to get there."

"Take him anyhow," Jericho said. "Keep a good grip on him. I don't trust him running around loose."

Lidi put her hand in Julian's. Old ghosts were stirring. She saw the same haunted look she had seen when they first met. All he had told her of the Baboon. And the whip scars. "You don't have to go there—"

"A matter of principle," Julian said. "I'm home again."

Behind her, the burning wagons had fallen in on themselves. Fire had scorched and blistered the painted lettering. There was nothing but charred timbers and drifting clots of ash. She looked back only once.

For what was left of the night, they cut across stubble fields and rutted tracks. Autumn dampness seeped into their clothing and chilled their bones. The stars had winked out; it was nearly dawn when Villa Malvento loomed in front of them at the end of a gravel-strewn carriageway. Muzio whined that his ribs hurt.

"Shut up," Julian ordered as they crouched in the tall weeds that had overrun the grounds. "I only want to hear one thing from you: Where did they put the girl?"

"I don't know, I swear, I swear," Muzio bleated. "That's the Baboon's business, he never told me. She could be anywhere—one of the sheds, the barn, the stables."

"Helpful," the canvasmaster said to Julian. "All we need to do is poke around the whole estate. Unless we knock on the door and say, 'Please, *marchese*, begging your pardon, but we're looking for a kidnapped little girl.' And what about your old friend there? Set him loose and he'll go bawling his head off and rouse everybody in earshot."

"Suppose we tear his shirt into strips and tie him up with them," Lidi put in. "Gag him and leave him in the bushes."

"Bang him on the head for good measure," Jericho said. "That would keep him quiet."

"No, no, I can help you." Muzio twisted around to Julian, who still had him by the collar. "*Amico,* I was always on your side, I'd have stood up for you. Terrible, what the Baboon did. But how could I go against him? I never let on, but I was with you—"

"He's lying," Jericho said.

"Of course," Julian said. "But he could be useful. I've never been to the villa, I don't know the outbuildings. If he shows us the Baboon's quarters, if we can get our hands on him—he's the one we want."

"I can't think of anything else," Lidi said. "Yes, the Baboon first. Then we improvise."

"If you remember," Julian said, "I'm good at that."

"You'd better be," Lidi said.

The sky had turned gray as they moved closer to the mansion. The gardens, Lidi saw dimly, had gone to seed; the marble steps of the portico were cracked and chipped, and the house itself looked in disrepair. The *marchese* did not live as grandly as she expected.

Muzio gestured for them to skirt the mansion and go to the rear. Lidi, about to follow, heard footsteps on the gravel behind her. A hand seized her by the hair, lantern light blinded her. She cried out and tried to break away. As Julian turned back toward her, Muzio tore free.

"They made me bring them here," he yelled. "They beat me, tortured me—that big brute worst of all. But I told them nothing, nothing."

He scrambled to the heavy-shouldered man holding the lantern. Lidi saw two other figures with muskets leveled. Julian sprang to her side. The man let go of Lidi's hair and squinted at him. He barked out a laugh.

"What's this? What's this?" said the Baboon. "Do I believe my eyes? Why, here's our runaway come back to us. I'd almost given up on you."

The Baboon took a pistol from his waistband. "So here

we are again, like the day you slunk off. Well, boy, who takes a bullet for you this time?"

The Baboon gave a lopsided grin. "You've just made my fortune. What do you say to that? Oh, yes, there's a reward still out for you, a big reward, and I'm the one to claim it."

"I brought him," put in Muzio. "I get a share."

"What you'll get is my boot in your behind," the Baboon said. "Clear out. Go tell the *marchese* he has company."

He swung back to Julian. "You give me a hard decision. You're wanted dead or alive; I'll have my reward either way. Which will it be? Dead, you're a lot less trouble; no courts, no magistrates, I shoot you now, all neat and tidy. On the other hand, if I turn you in, they'll do more than just hang you. Messy things. You'll be grateful when they finally string you up. I'd like to see that. What's your opinion, boy?"

"My opinion?" Julian looked squarely at him. "My opinion is: to the devil with you."

"Still the impudent *cafone*," said the Baboon. "But that's not the tune you sang when I tickled you with my whip. You'd have liked to kill me, but you had no stomach for it. What, boy, did you turn brave since you've been gone?"

"No braver than I was," Julian said. "Yes, I wanted to kill you, it was all I thought about. No more. Matteo and his friends have their own scores to settle with you, and so they will. You're not important to me now. You don't matter. You're nothing."

"You think so? We'll see." The Baboon cocked and aimed his pistol.

Julian did not move. Lidi saw the ghosts behind his eyes

were gone. The two men stood face-to-face. It seemed a long time. The Baboon spat and turned away.

"Take them inside."

With the Baboon following, his companions prodded their captives up the marble steps, through an unlit vestibule, and into a shadowy, high-ceilinged chamber. Ancestral portraits hung, dust-covered, on the walls. What had been elegant pieces of furniture stood rickety and threadbare. On a side table was a plate with chicken bones, a heel of bread, and an empty glass.

A man in an embroidered dressing gown poked at a skimpy fire in a fireplace the size of a small cave. He turned. Lidi caught her breath.

"Welcome," said Scabbia.

25

Silence

HE HAD PUT ON A LITTLE WEIGHT since Lidi last had seen him, but Scabbia still had the same look of a shabby ferret and bared the same yellow teeth. The dressing gown slopped around his shoulders, the skirts brushed the floor. He bobbed his head and smiled as if he were gnawing one of the chicken bones.

"Ah, signorina—"

"Weasel! Thief!" Lidi first thought to get her hands around Scabbia's neck and, after that, decide what else she could do to him. Julian pulled her back as the Baboon's men raised their muskets.

"No need to be disagreeable," Scabbia said cheerfully. "I

admit I didn't expect you. Fire can be so destructive. Since you're here: Welcome."

"Where's Daniella? Where's the *marchese*?"

"The child? In excellent hands, you may be sure. The *marchese*?" he added, preening. "He stands before you. Myself."

"What the devil are you telling us?" Jericho broke in. "You're as much a nobleman as I am. You twisting worm, I should have tied you in a knot as soon as I laid eyes on you."

"Hold your tongue. Don't try my patience," Scabbia said, with an edge to his voice. "You take me for some hole-and-corner moneylender? No. The Marchese di Malvento, as indeed I am."

"He can't be," Lidi murmured to Jericho. "Impossible."

"Money makes everything possible," Scabbia said. "It works more wonders than your little bag of tricks. My villa, my landholdings . . ." He waved a hand at the portraits on the walls. "Without putting too fine a point on it, I may call these my revered ancestors. Recently acquired, but mine even so.

"All at a bargain price, with the family crest thrown in. I bought it from the *marchese* himself—now the former *marchese*.

"He was delighted to sell. All the more since the old goat had no direct heir. As you see, the place has gone to ruin. I am in the process of refurbishing it. New furniture, draperies, fittings have been ordered—but, alas, not yet arrived. The tenant farms are in even worse condition. They barely turn a profit.

"That will soon change. The Baboon has assured me: Under his firm hand, with no tolerance of slackness, the farms will give a handsome return. And, better yet—"

"Don't tell me about profits you'll squeeze out of your tenants," Lidi broke in. "I met some people who mean to put an end to that. I want Daniella. Now. Hand her over, you disgusting little ferret."

"You don't understand," Scabbia flung back. "I *must* have the child. She's vital to my business. What a marvelous coincidence that she was seen here in Malvento. Oh, yes, I heard about it very quickly, and sent my trusty Baboon to get her.

"She set me on my way to a fortune, you know. Thanks to her, I could afford to buy this estate. Her prophecy—surely you recall it. She saw the grandeur in store for me: *Money will come into your hands. You will go far and rise high—*"

"It was nonsense," Lidi retorted. "It meant nothing."

"Everything! It meant everything!" cried Scabbia. "The prophecy came true. To begin, I found a purse—"

"Which wasn't yours," Lidi said. "You cheated a widow out of it. You must have guessed it belonged to Signora Antonia. It was the exact amount she owed."

"Neither here nor there." Scabbia waved it away. "Money came into my hands, as the child foretold. The foundation of everything that followed. With it, step-by-step, I was able to buy and sell, speculate, invest. Every new transaction brought greater profits than the last. Until, as you see, all this. Indeed, I've gone far and risen high."

"Be satisfied, then," Lidi said. "Let her go."

"I told you, once," Scabbia said between his teeth. "I get what I want. Give her back? Am I such a fool? This is only the beginning. No end of greater fortune to come, with her predictions to guide me. You should have done business with me when I offered. I'll rise higher yet. And you . . ."

He paused and pursed his lips. "You. Yes, a small difficulty. What a shame the fire didn't get rid of all of you. Ah, well, no matter. The Baboon will see to it.

"On the other hand," Scabbia said thoughtfully, "waste not want not. You may be useful to me."

"Not if I can help it," Lidi said.

"You'll be glad to. If you want the child to stay alive." He turned to the Baboon. "Bring them along."

"I want that one." The Baboon jerked a thumb at Julian.

"You most certainly shall have him," Scabbia said. "Once we're done, I give him to you. It pleases me to be generous."

Scabbia led the way from the room, through a corridor, and down a flight of stone steps. A wine cellar, Lidi saw it to be, with a vaulted ceiling, a wall of empty racks filmed with dust and trailing cobwebs. Candles guttered on a table. Shadows filled the rest of the chamber.

Daniella sat hunched on a stool. A length of heavy rope coiled around most of her small body. Her eyes were swollen, bruises smudged her cheeks. Seeing Scabbia, she cringed and turned her face away.

"Damn you, what have you done?" Lidi flung herself toward the girl. Scabbia snatched her arm.

"She's quite well, by and large," he said. "Do you think I'd harm my little goose who laid my golden egg?"

Daniella only now recognized Lidi. The child's lips moved. No words came.

"You see my difficulty," said Scabbia. "She won't speak. I've made every effort. The Baboon has tried his expert hand. Nothing. Another gentleman as well has made the attempt many times over.

"My dear cousin," Scabbia added as a figure, leaning against the wall, slouched from the shadows. "I sent for him when I took over the estate. I wanted him to share in my prosperity. Family, you understand. Blood is thicker than water. I trust him to keep my accounts and manage the daily details. He has been diligent at his work. In this case, how-ever, he has achieved no results."

The man grinned slantwise at her. His head tilted from one side to the other, nearly resting on his shoulders.

"Zaccovelli!" Lidi burst out. "He kept the inn—Daniella was there."

"Until you stole her!" Zaccovelli shook a fist. "You cheated me. I swore I'd get back at you. And here you are, and here she is.

"Cousin Scabbia told me about the brat. Worth more than I ever thought." Zaccovelli's head wobbled furiously. He jabbed a finger at his chest. "I was the one who saw you in Malvento. Lucky I did, or you'd have slipped away."

"For which you'll be well rewarded," put in Scabbia. "I've dreamed of finding the child. I knew, someday, I would. I knew, sooner or later, she'd be with me to see her prophecy come true, to witness all I've gained, my noble title, my estate—"

"You bought it," Julian broke in, "but, in the end, you won't keep it. Your land, by law, goes back to the tenants."

"You suggest I have no offspring?" Scabbia said. "Easily arranged. Naturally, I intend to marry. The matter will take care of itself. As the richest man in Malvento, I'll have my choice of eager brides."

He turned an eye on Lidi. "You yourself might consider the opportunity. To keep the family together, so to speak. No? I thought not. I make the offer, nonetheless.

"I'm a patient man," he went on. "By the time the child comes of age, she'll have been taught and trained to admire me, be devoted to me. She'll be delighted to join me in matrimony.

"A perfect match," Scabbia added. "We'll be the happiest of couples: she, telling me how to increase my wealth; I, reaping the benefits. At the moment, she stubbornly refuses to say anything at all."

"Of course not," Lidi said. "She's terrified. With Zaccovelli, she never spoke a word. And you? Look what you've done. Expect her to talk? She won't. She can't."

"This is where you may do me a service," Scabbia said. "You, surely, can calm her, persuade her. It would be to her benefit. And yours."

"After all she's gone through," Lidi retorted, "she may never speak again. Even if she does, I don't know what she'll say. Whatever gift she has, it may have left her."

"I sincerely hope not," Scabbia said. "If that's the case, she's useless to me. My little goose lays no more golden eggs? I would, alas, have to dispose of her. And you. She will speak. She must. Her life depends on it. Yours, too."

"It could take me a while," Lidi said, after a moment.

"I am, as I said, a patient man. Within limits."

"Another thing," Lidi added. "No harm comes to any of us."

"You're in no position to haggle," snapped Scabbia. He rubbed his chin. "I did promise the young man to the Baboon. He'll be deeply disappointed. But—yes, I agree."

"Don't believe him," Jericho burst out.

"She'll have to, won't she?" replied Scabbia.

"Untie her," Lidi ordered. "I can't do anything with her as she is."

Scabbia motioned for the Baboon to unwind the rope. Daniella still sat motionless. Her eyes were fixed on Lidi, who went to kneel beside her. The child's lips moved. Lidi bent closer, trying to catch the whispered words:

"Do the rope trick."

26

The Rope Trick

"I CAN'T," LIDI MURMURED. "I don't know how."

"Do the rope trick." There was no trace of fear in Daniella's voice. She looked intensely at Lidi. Her bruised face seemed alight. "Yes," she said. "Yes. Do it."

The rope lay on the flagstones where the Baboon had dropped it. Lidi snatched it up. The child's eyes were still on her. Lidi hesitated, her hands trembled.

"What's this?" burst out Scabbia. "What are you up to?" He started toward her.

"Stay back." Lidi did not recognize her own voice and its fierce tone of command. "Away from me."

Scabbia halted. The Baboon's men raised their muskets as Daniella sprang to her feet.

"*Now!*"

With all her strength, Lidi flung the rope at the vaulted ceiling. Scabbia sucked in a long breath. The Baboon's jaw dropped.

The rope hung in midair.

Zaccovelli gurgled like a bottle being emptied. The Baboon's men lowered their muskets to stare fearfully. The rope had gone taut, straightening to its full length, growing longer yet as it rose higher.

"Climb!" Daniella cried.

"Seize them, you cowards!" shouted Scabbia. "It's only a trick."

The rope battered against the vaulted stones of the ceiling. There was a loud grinding and crackling. The Baboon's men flung away their weapons and fled the cellar as jagged shards of masonry pelted down on them.

"Julian! Jericho!" Lidi called out. "Take Daniella!"

She swept up the child and practically tossed her to Julian. Daniella clung to his back as he seized the rope and hauled himself up. At Lidi's order, Jericho followed.

Lidi spun around to fend off Scabbia, who cursed and shouted for the Baboon. Jericho climbed steadily after Julian and the child. By now, the ceiling had broken open. The rope shot through the widening gap. Zaccovelli threw up his arms to shield himself from the hail of rubble. The Baboon staggered and pitched to the ground under heavy fragments of falling stone.

Daniella was calling to her. Lidi turned and gripped the rope. The whole cellar was collapsing; blocks of granite crashed around her. Through a swirling cloud of dust, she glimpsed the bodies of Zaccovelli and the Baboon half buried in the debris.

Only Scabbia was on his feet. As Lidi climbed beyond his reach, he sprang after her and clung to the rope. The upper floors of the house shattered one after the other and fell away. Scabbia, teeth clenched, heaved himself almost within arm's length of Lidi.

The roof broke open in an eruption of tiles; beams and rafters snapped like matchsticks. The rope sped upward, higher and higher into the sky. Wind shrieked in her ears. Beyond the clouds, stars whirled and scattered. She did not dare to look up or down. She was aware only of Scabbia still clinging below her.

In a black ocean, Lidi could not tell if her eyes were open or shut. It was brutally cold. Her hands felt frozen to the rope. Her sense of time had vanished, she barely remembered there had been such a thing. She had no idea how long she had been hurtling through darkness; it could have been moments or forever.

Suddenly the rope went slack. Lidi's heart lurched into her throat. She was falling. Daniella's voice came thin and faint:

"Let go!"

Lidi tore her hands away and went spinning head over heels. The rope, as it dropped, lashed around Scabbia. He plummeted downward. She heard him scream. After that, silence.

Water closed around her. She had plunged into a green sea. Rays of light filtered from the surface. Her feet scraped against sand. She stood up, waist-deep in the tide. Ahead, under a dazzling sun, curved a sparkling white beach; beyond it, foliage greener than any in Campania; farther yet, a long sweep of blue-hazed hills.

Jericho, surfacing, put his hands of his hips and stared around. "I thought I'd seen every kind of trick," he said. "Not this one. Do you mind telling me what you did to that rope?"

"Nothing," said Lidi, as baffled as the canvasmaster. "The rope did it to us."

Julian was next to her, holding Daniella. The child's face was no longer bruised, neither were her spirits. She laughed and clapped her hands. Something on the shore had caught her eye. She wiggled free and splashed her way to the beach.

"Come see the donkey," she called. "And the kitty."

As they waded after her, Lidi saw there was indeed a donkey. A black-and-white cat perched on its back. Beside them walked a man carrying a long staff.

He looked nothing like the descriptions Pompadoro and the others had given her, but she knew him instantly. She ran to him.

"Ferramondo," she said. It was not a question.

"So you found me." The man smiled. "I thought you would. In fact, I was expecting you."

"I can't say we were expecting you," put in Jericho as he and Julian caught up with Lidi. "Much as I hate to admit it—all right, I'm surprised. After what we went through, I'm surprised we're still alive." He added, uneasily, "If we are."

"Oh, yes, very much alive," Ferramondo said. "More alive than you ever were."

"But—what is this place?" Lidi pressed. "How did we get here?"

"You went through the threads," Ferramondo said. "As I told Pompadoro—go beyond the threads and everything's possible. Here? Quite a remarkable place, altogether fascinating. You'll be amazed at what there is to see and do. I doubt that anyone's come to the end of it. But you'll want to find that out for yourselves."

Daniella, frisking with the cat, had come to Ferramondo. "Are there piggies, too?"

"Of course," Ferramondo said. "All the animals. You've met my donkey, Aceto—he got here before I did and the dear old fellow waited for me. Pistachio and I arrived together. Go along with them. They'll show you whatever you like."

"I'll take your word this is all you say it is," Julian broke in. "Now, how do we get back to Campania?"

"But you just got here," Ferramondo said. "Going back? That would be rather difficult, a trick even I haven't learned yet. Don't worry. You'll be so busy discovering things you never imagined, you won't want to leave.

"Thinking of your lads from Malvento, are you?" he added. "They'll win out, in the long run. Thanks to you. What you began, they'll finish. They won't forget you, either. They'll make you a hero whether you like it or not.

"Apart from that," Ferramondo went on, "I daresay you have all you could wish."

"Yes." Julian took Lidi's hand. "All."

"I'll add something," Jericho said to him. "I once told

you I'd disconnect you joint by joint. I take that back. I give both of you my blessings."

"A lovely gift," said Ferramondo. "Now you needn't play at being a sour-tempered old canvasmaster. Come along. Daniella will be far ahead of us."

"Ferramondo . . ." Lidi drew him aside. "You said you expected us. How did you know?"

"I didn't," Ferramondo said. "I guessed. I'm very good at guessing. Had I known ahead of time—well, I'd be the Added Attraction, wouldn't I?"

"Who are you, then? Really."

"Really?" Ferramondo laughed and shook his head. "Sometimes I wonder about that myself. Let's just say: a magician. That's good enough."

"And the rope trick? You're the only one who can do it. But I did. How? I don't understand. I wanted to learn it more than anything. And never found the secret. Will you tell me?"

"Dear child," Ferramondo said, "you already know it."